Man vs. Durian

Baldwin Village, Book 3

Jackie Lau

First edition: August 2019

Print ISBN: 978-1-989610-01-5

Edited by Latoya C. Smith, LCS Literary Services

Cover by Jay Pillerva

Prologue

Peter

Ten years ago...

"What's that smell?"

This is not what a guy wants to hear when he's about to have sex for the first time.

To be clear, the smell isn't me. I'm absolutely certain of that. I was careful to shower and put on deodorant before I took Deepti out for dinner.

We've been planning this night for a while. Dinner at a not-so-fancy restaurant—we're first-year university students, after all—before coming back to my dorm room to get it on. We've been together for three months, and we've fooled around a *lot*, but this is the night. I bought condoms and a box of chocolates, and we've been feeding each other chocolate as we strip down.

And now, we're naked...and she's complaining about a smell.

I know exactly what she's talking about. I can smell it, too. Gas and vomit, I think—so, two different smells. They don't go well with romance, and I'm annoyed with whoever has already drunk enough to puke at nine o'clock on a Saturday. The gas is curious, though.

But I wasn't going to say anything. Because, you know, the whole having-sex-with-my-girlfriend business. I'd decided I could put up with the smells.

"I'm sure it's nothing," I murmur, kissing my way up Deepti's neck before popping another chocolate in her mouth.

She shakes her head. "I think there might be a gas leak."

"Mm." I kiss just below her jaw, where she's ticklish. "Don't worry about it."

"A gas leak, Peter!"

She's right. It could be a gas leak, but I have more important things to worry about. Like the naked girl in my bed.

However, I want this to be good for her. It'll be her first time as well. And, yeah, it smells pretty bad.

I stand up and put on my clothes. "I'll see what's happening out there."

I've just put my hand on the doorknob when the fire alarm goes off.

"Oh my God!" Deepti shrieks. "Where's my shirt?"

I locate her shirt and throw it over. She gets dressed in a hurry, then we pull on our winter coats and boots and hurry downstairs.

There's a large group of students outside, in various stages of drunkenness and undress, and from all the conversations, I gather that someone pulled the fire alarm because they were certain there was a gas leak, and gas leaks are dangerous things.

"It's like my mother knew what I was going to do," Deepti whispers, "and did her best to prevent it. But a gas leak is pretty extreme."

The fire trucks arrive, and the firemen rush into the building.

We wait. And wait. It's the middle of January, and it's fucking cold. I wrap my arms around Deepti, trying to keep her warm, but our teeth are chattering.

Finally, we're allowed back into the building, and we learn the source of the smell. It was not, in fact, a gas leak.

No, it was a durian.

Yes, that's right. My residence was evacuated because of a *fruit*. A goddamn fruit foiled my plans to get laid.

Now, I've eaten durian before. Once, I tried durian pancakes in Hong Kong. Just a bite because I would have gagged if I had any more. I don't know how people can enjoy something that smells so bad. It tastes the way it smells, too.

Who was the first person to try durian? What motivated them to look at a large fruit covered in giant spikes and think, "I wonder if that's tasty?" What inspired them, when they split open the fruit and discovered it smelled like utter shit, to put it in their mouth?

It's a mystery to me.

Some people like durian, though. They go on about how it's like the most heavenly custard, blah, blah, blah.

I don't understand those people.

Me, on the other hand...I never liked durian, and now it's cock-blocked me.

Ugh, that sounds crude. I care for Deepti very much, and I wanted tonight to be romantic, but now, the mood is ruined and she's thinking about her mother.

We return to my room and watch a movie, which isn't so bad because I still get to spend time with her, but dammit. I had plans.

We finally have sex the following weekend.

And durian and I? Fortunately, we don't have any further interactions.

Not for another ten years...

Chapter 1

Valerie

It's two in the morning, and I'm waiting for my mother to come home.

This is not the way things are supposed to be. I'm twenty-six years old. *I'm* the one who should be out late having fun, but I spent the evening watching Netflix in my pajamas.

After a few years of living away from my parents, it's been an adjustment to move back in with them and my younger sister. But after everything that happened last year, it was the best option, unfortunately.

And then two months ago, my mother retired.

Ever since, she's been determined to have the time of her life. Late nights playing mahjong are a regular occurrence. I mean, they were before, too, but not to the same extent. She'd always been home by freaking two o'clock in the morning.

I make myself another cup of tea and waste some more time on my phone.

It's two thirty now, and my mother *still* isn't home.

Two thirty on a Monday, that is. Monday's my day off, and now that Mom's not working, days of the week don't matter to her.

How did it come to this? My sixty-year-old mother has a more exciting social life than I do. I feel pathetic.

A common theme in my life these days.

I send my mother another text. I've been sending her texts once an hour since midnight. I don't think anything bad has happened to her, but this is rather disconcerting.

Finally, at three fifteen, I hear the key in the lock and breathe out a sigh of relief. My mom comes in, slips off her shoes, puts on her slippers, and tiptoes into the kitchen.

"Why are you still up?" she asks.

"You know I can't sleep until you get home." My father and my sister are sound asleep, but for whatever reason, I'm unable to rest if anyone in the household is out. It's annoying. I feel like *I'm* the mother. "What's that in your hand?"

My mother, who had been so careful to tiptoe through the house, slams a piece of paper down on the table. "I got a parking ticket!"

"What did you do? Park in front of a fire hydrant again? Mom, I *told* you—"

"Don't be silly! Of course I didn't do that. I learned my lesson the first time. Besides, I wasn't parked in front of that fire hydrant, just too close to it."

"Same difference," I mutter.

She waves the ticket in the air. "Apparently, you cannot park on the streets in Markham after two thirty in the morning. What a silly rule!"

"Maybe you should consider not staying out until three fifteen in the morning and have some mercy on the daughter who always waits up for you."

"That's your problem, not mine. Plus, I stayed up until three waiting for you to come home when you were in high school. This is payback!"

I sigh. "That only happened once. On prom night. I was very good at being home by eleven when I was in high school and university."

I went to the University of Toronto, so I was able to save money while doing my degree by living at home. I moved out as soon as I was finished, though. Stephen and I got an apartment together in the west end, far from my parents' house in Scarborough.

I push Stephen out of my mind. That asshole isn't worth my brain power. I still can't believe I gave him so many years of my life.

"You were not as good as you seem to think," Mom says.

I roll my eyes. "I was a very good daughter."

"What about now? You work at an ice cream shop! You're wasting your degree!"

Not this again.

I have a degree in computer science, and I used to work as a software developer. I was a damn good one, too. And then a whole bunch of shit happened. Shit that can be summed up quite succinctly: men are assholes.

"I told Minnie we could set you up with her nephew," Mom says. "Remember Kent?"

"Yes," I say with a sigh. I've met him a couple of times.

"He is studying to be an optometrist. I think he would be good for you. Encourage you to pursue your career in software development again."

"I don't want to be set up with Kent."

First of all, I am completely off men at the moment and have no interest in dating. Second of all, I don't think Kent is attractive. Third of all, he has bad breath. Fourth of all, he's an entitled brat. Fifthly, going out with Auntie Minnie's nephew sounds like an absolute nightmare. She and Mom would interfere non-stop.

And I can't return to software development as easily as Mom thinks.

She sniffs. "Well, lucky for you, Minnie refused to set you up. She's concerned you would distract him from his studies, plus she doesn't think you're good enough for him."

Although I have no interest in Kent, that hurts.

You know what? It's goddamn three thirty in the morning and I stayed up late to wait for my mother. I'm feeling tired and cranky and pathetic...

"I already have a boyfriend."

It pops out of my mouth before I can think about what I'm doing.

That's right, I just invented a boyfriend.

"You have a boyfriend and you didn't tell me?" Mom screeches, probably loud enough to wake everyone up.

"We haven't been together long. That's why I didn't say anything before."

"What's his name? Where did you meet him? What does he do?"

"His name's Peter." Why is that the first name that comes to mind? Probably because I watched *To All the Boys I've Loved Before* tonight. "We met at Ginger Scoops. He's a doctor." Of course he is. He's my fake boyfriend, so I might as well go all out and say the thing that will make Mom happiest. "Well, he's doing his residency right now. In pediatrics."

Yep, I'm dating a pediatric resident who nobly goes around saving children and puppies and God knows what else.

"I don't see him very often," I say. "Because, you know, he's doing his residency. He works all the time. That's why you haven't noticed me going out more than usual."

"Is he Chinese?" Mom asks hopefully. She would be okay with me dating a guy of any background, but she does have a slight preference.

"Yes."

She grins. "Wait until I tell Minnie!"

"You see?" I say. "If Peter is interested in me, I'm good enough for Kent Lo. But it's too late. I'm taken."

"When can I meet him?"

"Not anytime soon. Like I said, he's pretty busy."

And with that, I head upstairs to bed.

When I wake up at nine the next morning, my head is hurting and I'm full of regret, even though I didn't drink a drop of alcohol last night. But I didn't get enough sleep, and my late-night impulse to make up a boyfriend immediately rushes back to me. I trudge downstairs and pour myself some coffee. My mother is talking animatedly in Cantonese to someone on the phone, boasting about how her daughter is dating a doctor.

Dear God. What have I started?

"Valerie!" She smiles at me and puts down the phone. "Come sit!"

"How many people have you told about Peter?"

"Oh, just Minnie and Daphne and Connie."

So basically half the city will know by the end of the day.

I don't know how my mother has so much energy. She was up as late as I was last night, yet somehow she woke up earlier than me and seems quite perky.

"You have to tell me all about your boyfriend," she says. "What's his last name? Who are his parents? Aiyah, I know almost nothing! Cannot brag properly."

God, I have a headache. "This is why I never tell you anything! I say one word and the whole world knows about my life."

"Invite him over. Please. I promise to be good."

I snort. "Look, Mom, we all know that's a lie."

My sister, Sabrina, walks into the kitchen. She doesn't have class until eleven on Tuesdays. "What's this? Valerie has a boyfriend?"

"His name is Peter and he's a pediatric resident," I say morosely.

"He sounds boring. I bet he's ugly."

"Why do you assume he's ugly?"

"Past experience."

My sister thought Stephen was bad-looking. Not that I'm going to defend Stephen now.

"Peter is very good-looking," I say, raising my chin. If I'm going to have a fake boyfriend, he might as well be hot, right?

"He probably doesn't exist," Sabrina says.

Well, she's right on the money, not that I will admit it.

"Show me a picture," she says. "Surely you have one on your phone."

I slam my coffee mug down on the table. "I'm going to work."

"I can't believe you made up a boyfriend!" Chloe Jenkins says during a lull at Ginger Scoops.

Although it isn't busy right now, we had a pretty good summer, and I'm happy for my best friend. This is her business; I'm just working for her.

I look around the cutesy ice cream shop. It's clear she did the decorating, not me. There are rainbows and unicorns and alpacas and a bright pink wall.

Not my thing, in other words.

But I have my reasons for working here, even though any job that involves dealing with the public makes me want to stab myself with the horn of that rocking unicorn. People are just so damn annoying and inconsiderate.

I miss sitting in front of a computer all day.

"I can't believe it, either," I say. "Mom was going on about her friend's nephew being too good for me, and I felt pathetic. Now I feel even more pathetic for making up a boyfriend."

"You're not pathetic." Chloe touches my shoulder. "But what are you going to do? If only there was a chance your mother would forget, but she won't."

"Plus, she's already told everyone she knows." I feel bad for complaining about my mother in front of Chloe, since her mother passed away when we were twenty. "I suppose I'll make up stories about him for a week or two, then say we broke up." I shrug. "Whatever. How was your dinner last night?"

Chloe and her boyfriend, Drew, have been together for a few months, and she recently moved in with him. Chloe has always been the cheerful sort, but she's seemed happier since she started the ice cream parlor, and since she started dating Drew a couple of months later, even if Drew is a little grumpy, like me. He's good to her. For her.

"We went to that new izakaya," Chloe says. "It was pretty good. A bit loud, though."

The chimes above the door tinkle and Sarah Winters, who owns Happy as Pie across the street, walks in. "Do either of you want to go for laksa?" she asks. "There's a two-for-one special today." Paulie's Laksa, an Indonesian restaurant, is one of the other businesses in Baldwin Village. It's a few doors down from Ginger Scoops.

"Mm," Chloe says. "I'll go, if that's okay?"

"Sure," I say. "I'm not hungry." Not even for laksa, though I usually love the spicy noodle soup.

Sarah raises her eyebrows. "You okay?"

"My mother didn't get home until after three because she was playing mahjong, and then, in a fit of inspiration or stupidity, I made up a boyfriend. So, you know, everything's peachy." I bet this is evident from my monotone.

"Are you sure you don't want to go?" Chloe asks.

"Yeah, it's fine. Someone needs to stay. I'll do it."

My friends head out the door and I stare blankly at the rainbow painted on the wall. I'm not in the mood for laksa, but maybe I'll treat myself to durian ice cream when I take a break later this afternoon. I try to limit myself to eating ice cream once a week, and I haven't had any since last Wednesday. After the crappy night I had, I figure I'm due.

Durian ice cream won't make all my problems go away, but at least it's something.

Chapter 2

Peter

"Wʜᴀᴛ's ᴛʜᴀᴛ sᴍᴇʟʟ?" Cᴀʀsᴏɴ asks after he steps out of the truck.

Carson and I work for a small landscaping company whose main clients are rich people with mansions in midtown Toronto. We're currently at a house on the Bridle Path. It's owned by Brian Poon, who comes from some super-wealthy Hong Kong family.

Although it's the middle of September, it feels like a hot day in July. I'll be sweating buckets once we get to work on the hedges, but I don't mind. I like working outside.

I climb out of the truck and grimace. "Damn, that's pretty bad."

"It smells like a gas leak," Carson says. "What do you think?"

I hurry down the long flagstone path, past the fountain—rich people and their fountains—and knock on the door. Brian Poon's home is truly something to behold, and rumor has it that he hosts orgies on a regular basis, but I've never been able to confirm those rumors.

There's no answer, and oh dear God, the smell is getting worse. It smells like gas, as well as garbage, rotten onions, vomit, and...

Oh. I know exactly what it is.

"It's not a gas leak," I say to Carson as I head back to the truck. "Pretty sure it's durian."

"What the fuck is durian?" asks my white colleague.

"It's a fruit."

"No fucking way is that a fruit."

"I'm ninety-nine percent sure it's durian."

"You're shitting me. I know what gas smells like. That's gas."

"I'll call the client and see," I tell him. "Probably a good idea to check."

Five minutes later, I have confirmed that the smell is, indeed, durian. Apparently, Brian Poon had a party last weekend and there was durian involved. He didn't say anything about it being a durian and sex party, but that's what I'm picturing. I recently heard that durian is an aphrodisiac, which made me laugh my ass off. It sure didn't work that way for me back in university.

"If they ate all this fruit a few days ago," Carson says, "how come it still smells?"

"Behold, the magic of durian." I pull off my shirt and wrap it over my mouth and nose.

"You really plan to work in these conditions?"

"We have a job to do, and I expect it'll still smell tomorrow. Might as well get it over with."

I plan to work as fast as possible, then get out of here. Later this afternoon, I'll have a nice cold IPA and maybe some ice cream. There's a Thai rolled ice cream place that I like, not far from my apartment, as well as an Asian ice cream place in Baldwin Village that I've been meaning to try.

Yes, I love my ice cream, and after working in a durian-infested yard, I'll have earned it. The good thing about this job is that although I work hard during the day, the work never comes home with me, and I can enjoy my life. I have time to hang out with friends and go out with a girlfriend. When I have one, that is. I'm not seeing anyone right now, but I like being in a relationship.

I'm about to get the hedge trimmer out of the truck when my phone buzzes.

It's my father.

Okay, I can take this, but I'll make it quick.

"Hey, Dad, what's up?" I ask.

"I have a question for you," he says. "You ever been to that beach on the Toronto Islands? Hanlan's Point, I think it's called."

I scrub my hand over my face. "No. Why?"

"Your mother and I are thinking of going tomorrow. It's supposed to be hot again."

God, I really don't want to have this conversation, but it needs to be said.

"Dad, Hanlan's Point is a clothing-optional beach. You realize that, right?"

"Yes, I know. That's the point."

I was afraid of that.

Most of my Asian friends have trouble believing me when I tell stories about my parents. "Are you sure you're Asian?" they'll ask. "Because no Asian parent would not care about your grades and support you majoring in English. Or keep condoms in the bathroom from the time you were fourteen. Or offer to smoke pot with you. Or have no problem with your job in landscaping."

I guess it's partly because both of my parents grew up in Canada. They wanted to be "cool" parents. My mother's parents were quite strict, and she was determined to be the opposite.

"Why are you asking *me* about a clothing-optional beach?" I say.

"Just thought it was the sort of thing you might have done and was curious to hear—"

"Even if I'd been, why would I want to talk about the experience with my father?"

My dad laughs.

"Dammit, you asked that question just to piss me off!" Usually, I wouldn't be so irritated, but due to the durian picnic business, I'm not in the greatest mood.

"But we really are thinking of going to Hanlan's Point," Dad says.

"Yeah, yeah, do whatever you want. Just don't tell me about it."

I end the call.

Yep, I definitely deserve some ice cream today.

I live in a one-bedroom apartment in a condominium building in downtown Toronto. My parents bought it as an investment before real estate prices skyrocketed, and I pay them rent.

When I get home, I take off my dirty clothes and jump in the shower. Then I head to Ginger Scoops, the ice cream place in Baldwin Village. Time to try something new.

However, I've just stepped onto the patio of the ice cream shop when my phone buzzes. I stop walking and I pull it out of my pocket. There's a message from my father.

> DAD: Just wanted to inform you that Hanlan's Point has a "normal" beach in addition to the clothing-optional section.

Well, I'm thrilled to be enlightened. I—

I'm nearly knocked off my feet when a woman barrels into me.

We reach out to steady each other. She's holding an ice cream cone, though most of the pink and yellow ice cream is now on my shirt.

"Shit. Fuck. Goddammit."

I can't lie: I'm charmed by how vehemently she swears. She has long, shiny black hair, and her face is scrunched up. Still, I can tell it's a beautiful face.

"*Dammit.* I'm so sorry," she says. "I wasn't looking where I was going."

"I'm sorry. I was looking at my phone and…"

My voice trails off as I register a familiar smell. Natural gas and garbage and vomit and rotten onions. Like every terrible smell in the world has been combined into one, in the form of a menacing spiky fruit.

The durian.

"Is that durian ice cream?"

"Yes," she says, "and the pink one is red bean mooncake."

I whip off my shirt.

The instant I hear that I have durian on my clothes, it's my instinct to take off the piece of clothing. Not that this has ever happened before, but God, I want it as far away from me as possible.

If only it had been orange juice, like in *Notting Hill*, or bubble tea, or literally anything but durian.

My God, I feel like I'm cursed today. Cursed by durian.

Except this woman is really pretty, and she's staring at my naked torso with a strange expression on her face. I think it's an expression of appreciation, but it's mixed with something I can't quite identify.

I give her a sexy grin. "How about I buy you another ice cream?"

"No need. I work here. I can have it for free, and I'll get one for you, too. Come in and you can get cleaned up." She starts walking to the door, gesturing for me to follow.

"What's your name?" I ask.

"Valerie."

"I'm Peter."

She stops and turns around. "Your name is *Peter?*"

Chapter 3

Valerie

"Yes," he says, looking amused. "My name is Peter."

I know it's weird to be suspicious he doesn't know his own name. It's just...what are the odds? At three thirty in the morning, I made up a Chinese boyfriend named Peter, and a mere fourteen hours later, I spilled my durian ice cream on an East Asian man named Peter.

Not only that, but he's reasonably attractive and about my age.

He doesn't look like a pediatrician, that's for sure. If he were doing his residency, he wouldn't have enough time to work out on a regular basis, would he? This guy definitely looks like he goes to the gym, or maybe he has a job that helps him build those muscles...

Stop it, Valerie!

I open the door to Ginger Scoops, and he follows me inside.

God, what a rotten day. I'd been looking forward to my ice cream all afternoon. A group of university students arrived soon after Chloe left to get laksa, and they kept changing their minds about what they wanted, then sat in the corner and had a loud, annoying conversation. After that, a creepy old guy came in...

Anyway, it hasn't been a good day, especially since I didn't get enough sleep last night. That's probably why I wasn't looking where I was going and crashed into him.

How stupid of me.

I motion him toward a table near the counter. "Chloe, get him whatever he wants, on the house. I just spilled my ice cream on him." I turn back to Peter. "How about you give me your shirt and I'll rinse out the stain for you?"

He hands over his T-shirt and I head to the washroom. I'm able to get most of the stain out, and when I return, Chloe gestures me to the back room.

"He's handsome!" she whispers.

"You already have a boyfriend," I point out.

"Not for me. For you."

I roll my eyes. "You know I'm not interested in anyone."

"But you met in the cutest way. Just sit with him and see where this goes."

My God, Chloe has become an insufferable romantic.

"His name's Peter," I mutter.

"Ooh, like your fake boyfriend! It was meant to be."

"Please stop taking whatever happy pills you're on."

"Come on!"

"Fine, fine. I'll sit with him. But nothing's going to happen."

We head back into the shop. Chloe scoops out another durian and mooncake ice cream cone for me, and I walk over to Peter's table.

"Here's your shirt," I say.

He smiles at me, then licks his ice cream cone. He's got matcha cheesecake and ginger ice cream, and his tongue...

No, I am not going to think about what his tongue could do for me, or how I could use my own tongue on him. I have zero interest in men and dating right now. Men might have their uses, but they're bound to fuck you over eventually.

I learned that the hard way.

Peter still hasn't put on his shirt. I force my gaze up to his face.

"How's the ice cream?" I ask.

"It's really good, although I can't imagine the durian is tasty." He makes a face as he gestures at my cone.

"You don't like durian?"

"What's there to like? It smells awful."

"Oh, you're one of *those* people."

"I'm hardly alone," he says. "I suspect most people don't like durian. I mean, the smell is like a cross between a gas plant and a sewage plant, with some eau de vomit thrown in for good measure."

I chuckle. "I admit it's pungent, but—"

"Pungent? Is that a synonym for sewage treatment plant?"

"I don't mind the smell. In fact, it makes me smile because I know I'm about to eat something wonderful. Have you ever actually eaten it?"

"I have. I'm not a picky eater, but durian defeated me."

"It's so creamy. Like delicious fruit custard." I lick my ice cream and sigh in bliss.

He looks at me with a peculiar expression, then shakes his head. "Believe it or not, this was my second encounter with durian today. The man whose house I was working at this afternoon...he recently had a party, and there was durian."

"Sounds like a good party."

Peter glares at me, but it's a fond sort of glare, which is...odd. "Why would anyone want to be at a party where they served food that smelled like natural gas and hockey equipment? God, no."

"Just a few minutes ago, you described it as a cross between a gas plant and a sewage plant. Make up your goddamn mind."

"I like when you swear."

"Why the hell is that? Do you find it fucking adorable?"

He shrugs and has another lick of ice cream. "You do it with such passion."

"The first three words I said to you were 'shit, fuck, goddammit.'"

"Don't worry, I remember."

"Wait, are you flirting with me?"

He leans back in his chair, a smirk on his face. "Would you like that?"

I don't answer. To my embarrassment, I don't actually mind.

"I ran into you while carrying a durian ice cream cone," I say, "and you hate durian."

"I know." He shrugs again.

I expect him to trot out a terrible line. Something like, *I got to meet you, so it's all good.*

But he doesn't. He just sits here in Ginger Scoops, casually licking his ice cream cone, and he's still shirtless, for God's sake. How did I get into this weird version of reality?

Oh, and his name is Peter. Like my fake boyfriend.

Except I imagined my fake boyfriend to be an intense workaholic, and the man who's sitting before me doesn't strike me as a workaholic at all. Instead, he has a chill, easy confidence. Not an overly-inflated ego, just a nice level of confidence, which allows him to sit shirtless—

"Aren't you going to put on your shirt?" I say.

"Not sure I can do that. Kind of hard to get dressed while eating an ice cream cone."

"I'll hold your ice cream." I stick out my hand, and he passes it over.

"Just don't infect it with your durian ice cream," he says, pulling the shirt over his head.

"Don't worry, I'm not going to waste any durian on you."

He laughs as I hand back his ice cream.

Alright, much better. He's fully dressed now.

Except there's a wet spot where I washed ice cream out of his shirt. A rather large spot, about the size of my phone, over his nipple.

He just smiles at me. That bastard.

"You said you were working at someone's house," I say. "What do you do?"

"Landscaping."

I picture him working shirtless, dirt on his hands...

Nope. Don't go there.

This man is making me flustered, and I'm not used to this. I've been so in control of everything lately, making sure nobody screws me over again.

"Go out with me?" He just tosses it out there casually.

"No."

"Alright."

He doesn't push, and I appreciate that. Some men are really bad at taking no for an answer, but he's taking it all in stride, rather than redoubling his efforts because he sees me as a challenge.

Just then, my phone buzzes. It's a message from my mother.

> MOM: Please invite Peter over for dinner this week. I know he's busy, but I hope he can spare one night to meet your family.

I look up at the Peter sitting across from me, and an awful idea forms in my brain.

"How would you like to be my *fake* boyfriend?"

Chapter 4

Peter

A FAKE BOYFRIEND. Now that's a new one.

"What do you mean?" I ask.

"Last night I told my mom that I have a boyfriend named Peter," Valerie says.

"But you don't have a boyfriend?"

"Correct."

"So why did you tell her that?"

"Because she was going on about how I wasn't good enough for her friend's nephew, and she hates that I work in an ice cream shop. I was tired of her seeing me as pathetic and bugging me about my love life. It just popped out."

"Right."

"Don't judge me!"

"I'm not judging you." I eat the last of my ice cream cone.

"And now, here you are. Peter. What's your last name?"

"So."

"We won't even have to lie about how we met, since I said we met at Ginger Scoops. Just your profession."

"What does your fake boyfriend do?"

"He's a pediatric resident."

I chuckle. "Of course he is."

"It doesn't make a difference to me, but it had to be something that would impress my mother. So, pediatric resident it was."

"What would being your fake boyfriend involve?"

"First, we'd have to take a"—she cringes—"selfie together so I can show my mother."

The way Valerie cringes is kind of adorable. She's cute in a prickly way, and I like talking to her.

So I asked her out and she shot me down.

It happens. I was disappointed, sure, but she's just a woman I met fifteen minutes ago at an ice cream shop. In a very memorable way, true, and it's been many months since I've had the urge to ask a woman out, but we hardly know each other. I'd move on just fine.

Except then she asked me to be her fake boyfriend.

I'm intrigued.

It's the kind of thing I'd do just because it would make a good story. Besides, I wouldn't mind spending more time with Valerie, and maybe if I do a sufficiently good job at being her fake boyfriend, she'll go out with me for real.

And I have lots of practice at being a boyfriend.

"Sure," I say. "I'll be your fake boyfriend."

"You will?" she yelps.

"Yeah, why not?"

"You haven't heard what you'll need to do, other than the selfie. You'll have to meet my family."

"Okay."

"You'll have to be charming and pretend you're a doctor."

"Sure."

"If you want to date someone for real in the next couple of months, you'll have to keep a low profile. My mother will show your picture to all her friends, and my mom's friends always show up at the worst times, even in a big city like Toronto."

"Okay."

"We'll have to go on the occasional fake date. Preferably where someone I know will run into us."

"Sure."

Valerie sits back in her chair, looking stunned. "You're willing to do a meet-the-parents dinner for someone you don't even know? Why?"

I don't tell her all my reasons. I just say, "I'm doing it for the novelty of it. How often do you get to fake a relationship?"

"Look, I don't think you understand what you're getting into. My family is, um, nuts."

"I can handle it."

She seems doubtful but says nothing more about her family. "What other ridiculous things have you done?"

"I once had six slushies in an hour."

"Sounds sensible."

"I felt gross afterward."

"Naturally."

"I also danced all night in an inflatable T-Rex costume. And I did a polar bear dip. Went in Lake Ontario on New Year's Day."

She looks at me in absolute horror. Valerie has such a lovely expressive face.

"It was cold?" she asks.

"It was cold." My balls basically shriveled into peanuts, but I don't share that fun tidbit.

"I question your sanity."

"That's fair."

Suddenly, there's a wicked gleam in her eye. She leans forward, and I breathe in sharply at her nearness. "I've got another unusual thing you could do," she says quietly. It sounds seductive to my ears, but I don't think that's her intention.

Also, I can see a hint of cleavage, but I drag my eyes back up.

"Yeah?" I say, trying to remain calm. "What's that?"

"Eat a whole pint of durian ice cream."

"Absolutely not."

"I thought you were adventurous."

"I am. But we've established that I do not like durian, and I already have enough durian stories. There are two from today, for starters. And that time back in university…"

"Where did you go to school?"

"Queen's. For English. I guess you should know that if we're supposedly dating."

"Yes, but I'm going to lie and say your major was life sciences. Since you went to med school afterward, it makes more sense."

"Right, right. The doctor thing."

She twists her lips to the side.

I really need to stop focusing on her lips.

"Okay, no pint of durian ice cream," she says. "How about a sample? One teeny, tiny spoonful? Please?" She puts her hands together, as though pleading with me.

I'm a sucker for this woman, so I let out an exaggerated sigh. "Sure. But you better get me a coffee to wash it down."

She scurries behind the counter, where she exchanges some frantic whispers with another woman before she returns with a small pink spoon containing durian ice cream. "Here you go. Chloe will bring over the coffee in a moment."

I take the spoon from her hand and peer at it. The ice cream *looks* harmless, but I can already smell its terrible smell. Best to get it over with.

I wince as I bring the spoon closer to my mouth, and then I bite the bullet.

Yes, it's creamy and cold. Yes, it's slightly fruity.

It's also absolutely disgusting and I scrunch up my face as though I'm in pain.

"Cheese!" Valerie says, holding up her phone.

Well, I bet that's a great picture.

Thankfully, Chloe comes over with a coffee, and I grab it and take a gulp. It's hotter than I expected, but that's okay. Better for burning the taste of durian off my tongue.

"I can't believe you made him try durian ice cream," Chloe says. "Not everyone likes it as much as you do, you know."

"What can I say?" Valerie says blandly. "I'm evil."

But then she smiles, and I feel like it was all worth it.

My fake girlfriend might be a little evil, but I'm looking forward to this.

"Are you serious?" Aaron slaps his hand on the table and laughs. "You want to go out with this girl, but instead you agreed to be her fake boyfriend—which I assume doesn't involve any sexual benefits—and tried durian ice cream?"

Leon is also laughing hysterically.

"Thanks, guys," I say, lifting my pint.

Aaron Wyman and Leon Swartz are friends of mine from high school, and occasionally we get together for a few beers, usually at a sports bar not far from where I live.

"You've been single for, what? Six months?" Aaron says. "Getting desperate, are you?"

"Eight months, actually."

"When's the last time you were single for that long?"

I think for a moment. "When I was fifteen."

The truth is, I like being in relationships. Always have. I like romance. I like intimacy. There's nothing better than the first few weeks of a new relationship, but I also enjoy it when I've been with someone for a while and know all their quirks.

Alas, none of my relationships have lasted more than a year and a half, but I'm sure I'll get there someday. I'll find the woman I want to marry. It's just a matter of time, and I'm twenty-eight—I've still got time.

My friends used to say I was a serial monogamist, always jumping from one relationship to another, but I've gotten better at being single in the past couple of years. I no longer feel an uncomfortable itch when I'm single for more than a few weeks.

And, yeah. Eight months. That's a while.

I even managed to have a one-night stand a few months ago, which is out of character for me. I'm usually all about relationships.

"I wasn't *that* desperate," I say. "It took a while to find the right woman, that's all."

"You think a woman who force-feeds you durian ice cream—"

"Hey, she didn't force-feed me. I could have said no." But I was overcome with the urge to amuse her. Unfortunately, I now have photographic evidence of the moment when I looked like I was about to hurl—she sent me the picture, along with the couple's shot she took of us.

I keep looking at the second picture and smiling.

"I'll be the best fake boyfriend ever," I say, "and then, hopefully, she'll change her mind. If not..." I shrug.

Actually, the idea that she might not change her mind fills me with crushing disappointment. But there are other women out there; I'll pick myself up and keep going.

In about half of my relationships, I was the one who was dumped. Some weren't a huge deal, but three of them were pretty rough. In fact, my last relationship ended with me getting my heart broken, and that's part of the reason it's been eight months. For four months, I had no interest in another relationship.

But now, I'm back to my usual self, and I'm ready to try again.

And Valerie *was* checking me out when I had my shirt off, and she *did* ask me to be her fake boyfriend, so I figure she likes me at least a little. I'd been prepared to walk away, but her fake relationship plan?

I think that's a good sign.

Chapter 5

Valerie

"HE'S HANDSOME!" MY MOTHER says as she peers at the picture of me and Peter.

"He is," Sabrina admits grudgingly. "I don't believe that man is a fucking doctor."

"Don't swear!" Mom says.

"Valerie swears all the time!"

"Valerie is a lost cause."

"Thanks," I mutter.

Mom continues to stare at the picture. "I don't know what you have against doctors," she says to my sister. "People like doctors. *Grey's Anatomy*, right? Why couldn't one of you be a doctor? Ah, well, marrying a doctor is the second best thing."

Not gonna lie, the word "marry" freaks me out. I don't want to think about marriage. Just the idea of another long-term relationship scares the crap out of me.

No, I'm not going through that shit again.

Men just want to use me. They only care about what I can do for them, and when I stop being useful...

Well, they start being sloppy with their affairs.

I was so involved in my work—my actual job, plus the work I was doing for free for Stephen—that I was blind to what he was doing.

Nope, never again. I will never let another man pull the wool over my eyes like that.

I'm well aware that some women—like my friends—have good relationships, and I'm happy for them. Still, I'm convinced that every man who's interested in me is untrustworthy. Past experience and all that.

My brother, Alan, walks into the kitchen. He's eight years older than me, and he's an assistant professor in the earth sciences department at the university. He usually comes over for dinner on Wednesdays.

"What's this about marrying a doctor?" he asks.

"Valerie has a new boyfriend!" Mom shoves the phone in his face. "He's a doctor."

"Like me."

"Wah, not like you! PhD in geology is not the same as a medical degree."

Alan laughs. He likes saying that to annoy Mom.

Still, although he might not have done exactly what she wanted, my mother is proud of Alan. He's a professor. He has multiple science degrees. He's respectable.

Me, on the other hand...

I work at an ice cream shop.

She used to brag about me. I graduated second in my class at university, ahead of all the boys, and my mom was proud, even if she jokingly asked why I didn't come in first.

I got a job at an engineering software firm, and she approved of that, too. She wasn't pleased that Stephen and I were living together without being married; she thought I should live at home until we got married or, at the very least, engaged. But she didn't make too much of a fuss.

And then, over one horrible week last year, my job and relationship imploded. I'd hoped she'd have more righteous anger on my behalf, but she acted like it was partly my fault, and now she's pissed I'm working for Chloe.

Alan turns to me. "You have a boyfriend? I thought you weren't interested in dating again."

Yeah, he'll be harder to fool. My mom is lapping this up because it's exactly what she wants, but Alan knows me better than she does.

The horrible truth? Mom loves me because of what I can do for her. A daughter who's dating a doctor? She can brag about that. It makes her look good—and I haven't done anything to make her look good in a while.

I know she loves me beyond that, but sometimes she cares about other people's opinions a little too much.

"Yeah, I have a boyfriend," I say. "No big deal. What's new with you?"

Alan doesn't answer my question. "What's his last name?"

"Nope. We're not doing this. I'm not telling you his last name so you can google the shit out of him."

"Valerie!" Mom says.

"I thought you said I was a lost cause? Why do you care that I swear?"

Alan shoves his hands in his pockets. "This Dr. Peter better treat you well."

"Of course he will!" Mom says. "He looks like he's very sweet, and he has kind eyes."

"Pretty sure you said Stephen had kind eyes, too," I mutter. I have no idea what "kind eyes" means. Sounds like bullshit.

"You did," Sabrina says. "I remember."

"Kind and sweet," Mom says. "But still sexy."

"Mom!" Sabrina and I say in unison.

We don't agree on much, but neither of us wants to hear our mother say "sexy."

"Will you invite him over this week?" Mom asks. "Or we can go to a restaurant near the hospital if that is easier for him."

Hmm. I really need to give some thought to how long I want to continue this fake-boyfriend charade. I still can't believe he accepted. I was kind of joking, but then he agreed, and I thought...sure, why not?

It's nice that my mother is happy with me for the first time in ages, and I loved seeing the shock on Sabrina's face when she saw his picture. I'm having fun, even if my mom used the dreaded S-word and M-word.

"Sexy" and "marriage," I mean.

I still don't understand Peter's motives for agreeing to this—doing it all for the novelty of a fake relationship seems a bit much—but I have my eyes wide open, and I won't let him take advantage of me.

But although I initially came up with this plan when Mom suggested I have Peter over this week, I don't feel ready for that yet.

"Nope," I tell her. "He'll come over eventually, just not for a few weeks. I don't want to scare him off."

"I'm not scary!" Mom protests.

Sabrina snorts in response.

"Look," I say. "This is my first relationship since Stephen, and I'm taking it slow, okay? Meet-the-parents dinners are not happening right away."

"Hmph. You better not meet his parents before he meets us."

"Don't worry, I won't."

That's one promise I can keep. This entire charade is for the benefit of my family, not his. I doubt he's going to tell his parents that he has a girlfriend named Valerie.

·❤ · ❤ · ❤ · ❤ · ❤·

I can't wait until this day is over. My God.

I've been at Ginger Scoops since noon, and it's eight thirty now. Only half an hour left, and then I can get out of here.

My brain is numb and my feet hurt and I'm just generally frustrated with humanity.

At two o'clock, there was a crying baby. It wouldn't have been so bad if she'd just cried for a few minutes, but no, she wailed for half an hour while her parents stayed in the shop—they didn't take her outside.

At three o'clock, two large families made a complete mess of the back corner, and I had to clean it up.

At four o'clock, I went to clean the washroom and found it was a mess, too.

At five thirty-three, someone complained that their green tea ice cream was too "tea-y" and could they please exchange it for some passionfruit ice cream?

At six thirty, I dropped the ice cream scoop on my foot.

At seven o'clock, a creepy old man asked me on a date.

At eight o'clock, there was an honest-to-God family feud in the ice cream shop. A man and two women were arguing loudly, their children were fighting, and guess what? There was another crying baby, too.

When I first started working for Chloe, we were preparing Ginger Scoops for opening, so it was just the two of us. That was nice, after everything I'd been through. I was working with my friend and helping her dreams come true, and it was a relief not to have to use my brain.

But then we opened and I had to deal with customers.

Many of them are just fine. They tell me what flavors they want, they pay, they talk to each other as they eat, and then they leave. I don't get any pleasure out of serving them, but I don't mind.

And then there are the entitled assholes and the out-of-control children whose parents make no effort to rein them in.

And now...

"Oh, no," Chloe says. "Someone hurt Twinkle."

Twinkle is the rocking unicorn in the corner of our shop, except she now appears to be a rocking horse because her horn has been broken off. I don't know how I missed that.

"I'll superglue it back on," I say.

"It won't look the same."

"It'll be fine." I just want to get the hell out of here.

But today, I'm not going home after I finish my shift. No, I'm going to Cheese & Me with Peter. Our first "date."

I'm not excited. It's not a real date, after all.

Okay, maybe I'm a teeny-tiny bit excited, but that's it. More than anything, I'm ready to stop serving people who make giant messes and break off fucking unicorn horns.

Just after nine, Chloe's boyfriend comes in, and they do a little too much smooching by the front door. To my annoyance, I can't help some stupid envy from bubbling up inside me.

A couple of minutes later, Peter's face appears at the door, and I hang up my apron and gesture him inside.

He smiles at me. "You ready to go?"

"Yep."

"Who's this?" Drew asks.

"Peter. He's my fake boyfriend."

"I'll explain later." Chloe presses a kiss to her real boyfriend's cheek. "Wait here for a few minutes while I finish cleaning up."

"I'm so confused right now," Drew mutters.

As I follow Peter outside, I can't help smiling.

I'm just glad to be done work and going out for cheesecake, right?

That's all it is. It has nothing to do with Peter So.

·♥·♥·♥·♥·♥·

Cheese & Me is, not surprisingly, fairly busy. It's a Friday night, and there are lots of young people here, ready to stuff their faces with cheesecake and cheese tarts.

"Do you like Japanese cheesecake?" Peter asks as we wait in line. "Or are we just here to be seen?"

"I enjoy it."

But, yes. The reason I specifically asked him to accompany me to Cheese & Me is because Daphne's daughter Chrissy works here. She's a few years younger than me, finishing up her degree, and I know she works Friday nights. And if she sees me here with Peter, then she'll tell her mom, who will tell my mom, and my ruse will look real.

Yep, that's my devious plan.

We get to the front of the line and order some tea and a Japanese cheesecake. Unfortunately, the person taking our order isn't Chrissy, but Chrissy's the one who brings the tea and cheesecake to our table a few minutes later.

Excellent.

"Valerie!" she says in her too-loud voice that drives me bananas. "I haven't seen you in ages."

"Chrissy, this is Peter. My *boyfriend*."

Chrissy can only stay to chat for a minute, but that's okay. She's seen us. I've done what I wanted to accomplish.

Now it's time to eat. I turn my attention to the cheesecake, which is seven or eight inches in diameter, with a light brown top. I cut it in quarters and put one on a plate for Peter and one on a plate for me.

I pop a bite of the cake into my mouth. It's light and airy and not overly sweet, and I close my eyes to savor it. When I open them, Peter is peering at me curiously.

"What?" I ask.

He shakes his head. "Nothing."

"It was not nothing. It was something."

"No, it wasn't."

I grab his plate and pull it toward me. "Tell me."

He laughs. "Why does it matter?"

"I don't like it when people don't tell me things!"

"Alright." He scrubs a hand over his face. "I like watching you enjoy your food. That's all." He gives me a hesitant smile.

"Oh. Really?"

"Yeah."

Huh. Well, that was unexpected.

I push his cheesecake back toward him. He shifts his hand toward mine on the table, then immediately pulls back.

"Sorry," he says. "We haven't discussed physical affection. Like, can I hold your hand? Can I kiss you on the cheek? It would probably be best if we did a little of that, at least when the people you want to fool are nearby, but just let me know. I'm not sure of the protocol for fake relationships. If you don't want me to touch you at all, it's okay."

I laugh, but I appreciate this. I do.

"You can touch me in the ways you described. When we're in public." It's a bit loud in here, but that's good—it would be tough to overhear our conversation.

"What about this?"

A bite of cheesecake appears before my face.

Ah. He wants to feed me. I glance around the room and find Chrissy nearby, looking in our general direction. Perfect. As I lean forward, my heart starts beating a little faster, but it's not unpleasant.

Weird.

I eat the cheesecake from his fork. It's delicious.

"It's a good thing they didn't have durian cheesecake," he says. "I bet you would have insisted on getting it."

"Of course. I've never had durian cheesecake before. I can just imagine how amazing that would be."

"Bleh." He wrinkles his nose. "You'd probably get it all over my shirt somehow, and then I would stink."

"And you'd use it as an excuse to remove your shirt so you could show off your body."

"Are you saying you like my body?"

My cheeks heat. "You're decent-looking, and you clearly don't sit in a cubicle all day. That's just the truth."

The corner of his mouth kicks up, and ooh, that's rather sexy. I want to kiss him.

Oh my God, where did that come from?

Here's the thing. I find the thought of kissing a man I hardly know—a stranger at a bar, let's say—completely unappealing. I might find someone a little attractive at the beginning, but it always takes a while before I can even think of going further, before I can really feel sexually attracted to them.

But the idea of kissing Peter right now...it actually sounds kind of nice.

It's been a very long time since that's happened to me, and I'm thrown off by my reaction. He's just a guy.

We chat about nothing in particular and eat cheesecake for a little while. Peter is pretty easy to be with, actually, and I enjoy his light teasing.

I look at my watch. "It's getting late. I should head home."

"Sure. Let me ask for a box so you can take the rest with you." He gestures to the cake.

A few minutes later, we're walking outside in the warm-ish September air. I just survived my first "date" since the whole Stephen debacle. A fake date, but still. I'm pleased with how it went.

"Let's do something on Sunday," I say, before I know what I'm doing.

Peter agrees.

I head to the subway, shaking my head at the spur-of-the-moment decision to ask him out again. It's not like we need to see each other every two days to keep up this ruse, right?

When I get home, I'm practically tackled by my mother.

"Ah, you're smiling!" she says. "Good date?"

"It was."

"I heard you went to Cheese & Me. Daphne called to say Chrissy saw you there!"

Well, that was faster than expected.

"Yes, we went out for cheesecake." I lift up the box with the leftovers.

"Did he kiss you?" Mom makes loud smooching noises.

I glare at her. "I'm going up to bed."

Once I'm in bed, I do not think about Peter.

No, I most certainly do not.

Chapter 6

Peter

I want to make Valerie smile again. I'm addicted to her smiles.

I don't know where to find durian cheesecake downtown, but I do a little research on my phone and find the perfect thing to bring her for our next date.

I head to the bakery just before we meet on Sunday. In some ways, it's similar to the bakeries in Chinatown. You take a tray and a pair of tongs, and you put everything you want on the tray and bring it to the cashier.

Except here, rather than plastic cafeteria trays, there are smooth wooden trays lined with tissue paper, and the prices aren't "three for a dollar" but more along the lines of three to five bucks each. Expensive, in other words. There are smooth, flawless buns filled with things like red bean and taro. There are pineapple buns with their crunchy pineapple-less topping, like you'd get at a regular Chinese bakery, except these look like perfection, and they're actually "double pineapple" buns, filled with pineapple custard. I pick one up and put it on my tray. I better try something at the bakery and make sure it's good, right? Then I select another bun—the reason for my trip to this bakery. To my surprise, it doesn't smell.

The cashier gives me a little bag for my purchases, and I eat the double pineapple bun as I'm walking to Ginger Scoops. It's quite good.

Hopefully the other bun is just as good.

I don't know as much about Valerie as I'd like to, but from what I do know, I'm pretty sure she'll like this.

"I got you a present," I tell Valerie as we take a seat on the patio at Ginger Scoops. It's a Sunday, so it closed at seven. We're supposed to go out for dinner somewhere in the area.

"You didn't need to," she protests.

I shrug. "It's no big deal." I pull out the paper bag and set the bun on top of it. "For you."

"You got me a bun." She eyes me suspiciously.

"Yes. I got you a bun at a fancy-ass Asian fusion bakery."

"Is that what it called itself? 'A fancy-ass Asian fusion bakery'?"

"Actually, it was just called 'Eight Buns,' but it was fancy inside. Trust me."

"What is this?" she asks, nodding at the bun.

"Try it and see."

"Uh-uh. I'm not falling for that trick again."

"What have you been forced to eat in the past?"

"Rat poison."

"Who the hell fed you rat poison?"

"Sorry, sorry," she says. "I just mean, it could be filled with rat poison for all I know, but I'm sure it's something normal like barbecued pork."

"It's a durian bun, filled with durian custard. It's supposed to be the best durian bun in the city, and you deserve the very best in stinky fruit buns."

Her eyes light up...and there's that smile I was hoping for. It causes a pleasant warmth in my chest.

She picks up the bun. "Would you like to do the honors?"

"No, I'm not touching that."

She bites into the bun, closing her eyes. I've noticed that Valerie likes to close her eyes when she eats, as though it allows her to truly savor food.

"Good?" I ask.

For some reason, it's extremely important that she like it.

"Yeah." She sighs in bliss.

The extra stop before going to Ginger Scoops was definitely worth it.

There's a tiny bit of custard on her lip, and I want to lick it off. Then I remind myself that it's durian-flavored and must taste like absolute shit.

Still, I would happily lick her lip if she'd let me.

The key to romance, you see, is not bringing a woman dozens of red roses or hiring a string quartet to serenade her.

No, the secret is finding something that's uniquely for her, whether or not it's expensive.

She holds the bun out to me, and I instinctively turn away, fearing for the safety of my nose. I don't smell anything yet, but I'm sure the smell is there, now that she's bitten into it.

"Try it," she says. "Just a small bite. The durian isn't very strong."

"No?"

"Really, it's a mellow durian flavor."

"That's like saying something has a mild garbage flavor. I still don't want to eat it."

She makes a face, then thrusts the durian bun under my nose, but I stand up before I get a proper whiff of it. Valerie stands up, too, and I hurry around a nearby table. She follows. I dart around the next table and bang my knee on a chair.

"Come and get it," she says, shaking the half-eaten bun in her hand.

"I'm keeping my distance."

She doesn't move, so I stay where I am, my heart rate kicking up, not from scurrying around on the patio, but because of her. I enjoy being chased by Valerie.

"You sure you don't want this?" She grins and steps toward me.

I step back. "I'm sure."

"What kind of bribe would work on you?"

"Season tickets to the Leafs," I say automatically.

She rolls her eyes. "Oh, you're one of those rabid Leafs fans. You know, I've always thought the Leafs had an interesting business model. They put out a shitty product year after year, yet they're still one of the most valuable teams in the league. It's impressive."

"Maybe you missed the memo, but the Leafs are good now."

She shrugs and thrusts the durian bun toward me again. I try to step back, but I can't. I'm against the fence that separates Ginger Scoops' patio from the one next to it.

The next thing I know, Valerie is nearly pressed up against me and a mildly terrible smell permeates the air.

But she's pressed up against me. I'm intoxicated by her nearness...and the foul smell of the durian bun, but she's right, it's not nearly as bad as, say, the durian smell in Brian Poon's backyard.

"What are you two doing?" Chloe steps onto the patio. "It looks like you're trying to feed him a bun."

"It's a durian bun," Valerie explains.

When she looks at Chloe, I jump to the right. Away from Valerie, but also away from the foul-smelling bun. She chases me.

Chloe laughs and heads to the sidewalk. I can see her out of the corner of my eyes, but my focus stays on Valerie. Her mouth is open, and she's breathing a little quickly, and there's a wild look in her eyes that absolutely delights me.

I run to the other side of the patio and crawl under a table.

"What are you?" Valerie asks. "Five?"

When she crouches down next to me, it's like we're in our own little world, here under the plastic patio furniture. Some hair has escaped her ponytail, and I long to reach out and smooth it behind her ear, but I won't.

Because under the table, we don't have to fake it for anyone. It's just us.

And she only wants me to touch her in public.

"Come on," she whispers, and for a moment I imagine she's talking about something other than a freaking durian bun.

God, I want to touch her so badly. I want to toss aside that evil bun and press my lips against hers and pull her into my lap. I want to lie down on the ground with her on top of me, her breasts pressed against my chest.

But I won't.

I grin at her. "Eat the bun, Valerie."

"You got it for me. It's mine, and I can do what I wish with it. And I wish for you to try a bite." She holds it in front of my face again.

I should crawl out from under the table and stand up, but I like being in our own little world here. I like it a lot.

When Valerie shoves the bun under my nose again, I don't turn away. I smell sweet bun and fruity gasoline. Not that I've ever smelled fruity gasoline before, but I can imagine. I have a good imagination. For example, I'm currently imagining Valerie crawling across my bed in red lingerie, with a whole durian in her hand—

Wait. What the fuck? If it's a fantasy, why is there a durian in it?

"Try it," she says. "Just a tiny bite of the scrumptious durian bun."

"Geez, you're really pulling out the big words."

"I'm complimenting you on the present you gave me."

"How kind."

She holds the bun closer to my lips, and I lean forward. I admit I'm a bit curious to know what "mellow durian flavor" is like.

I take a small bite. The pleasantly-sweet bun is filled with some kind of custard, and it's not completely repellent. Like, I wouldn't buy one of these for myself, but it's not that gross.

"You didn't even make a face," she said. "You're a durian convert."

"Nope, not happening. But you're right, that isn't too strong."

We stand up and brush off our jeans, and for a moment, we simply stare at each other. It's almost dusk; the light is fading.

When night blankets the city, I want to be curled up in bed with her. Or maybe we'd chase each other around my bed with pillows. I don't know, but I want her there.

Except this isn't real, not really.

Not yet, anyway.

Valerie nibbles at her bun, and I keep my eyes on her lips, jealous of how something that smells of fruity gasoline gets to enjoy her lips.

"Are you still hungry for dinner?" I ask after she pops the last bite in her mouth.

She holds a finger up to indicate she's still chewing, then finally says, "Yeah, I'm hungry, don't worry. Where do you want to go?"

"Have you been to K-Polish?"

"No, actually, I haven't. Let's try it."

K-Polish is a Korean-Polish restaurant on Baldwin Street. We're quickly seated and given menus, which have a Korean section, a Polish section, and a fusion section. I read through the latter. There are bulgogi and kimchi pierogis, and potato pancakes stuffed with either kimchi jjigae or bulgogi with cabbage and pear. Then there's "sumptuous" soon tofu with "delectable" sauerkraut.

In fact, "delectable" appears three times on the menu.

And that's the first time I've ever heard someone refer to soon tofu as "sumptuous."

"What are you getting?" Valerie asks me.

"I think I'll have the 'sumptuous and scrumptious' potato pancake with kimchi jjigae. Though the last thing that someone described as *scrumptious* did not live up to the description."

She laughs. "I'm having the potato pancake, too, but with bulgogi. It's described as 'scrumdiddlyumptious,' so it must be better than yours."

I shoot her a look of mock outrage.

We place our orders, and our banchan arrives soon after. There are small dishes of kimchi and soybean sprouts, as one would normally get at a Korean restaurant, but there's also sauerkraut, as well as beet salad. I tackle everything with my chopsticks; Valerie uses her fork.

"We should get to know each other better," she says, "so I can answer my mother's numerous questions. She keeps bugging me about your family."

"Mom and Dad live in Thornhill. That's where I grew up. They were both born in Hong Kong but grew up in Canada, my mother in a small town near Ottawa, and my father in a small town near Waterloo."

"Do you speak Cantonese?"

"Very little."

"Well, that will make you a little less perfect in my mother's eyes."

"I'm sorry."

"No, thank God. It's getting annoying to be compared to you. She thinks you're, like, the perfect Chinese son and you go around saving babies all day."

I frown. "What?"

"You know. The pediatrician thing."

"Right, right. How could I have forgotten?"

"You better not forget on Thursday."

"Why, what's Thursday?"

"Sorry, I forgot to tell you." She deposits some kimchi in her mouth. "I've spent the past few days insisting it's too soon for you to come to dinner, but my mom wants to meet you, come hell or high water. She threatened to follow me around every day this week until she met you."

"Seriously?"

"Yeah. And since she's retired, she has the time to do so—I'm afraid it's not an empty threat. So I offered an informal meeting at Ginger Scoops on Thursday. She'll just come over and interrogate you for twenty minutes. I'll make sure it's no more than that. Anyway, you can keep all your personal details the same, for simplicity's sake. Except for your career, of course, and remember that you majored in life sciences. I'm sure you'll do fine."

"I've done the meet-the-parents thing many times before."

"How many?"

I think for a moment. "Ten?"

"Ten different women?"

"Yeah."

"*Ten?*"

I shrug. "I've had thirteen girlfriends."

Her eyes bug out of her head. "*Thirteen?*"

"Polly, is that you?"

She screws up her face.

"You sound like a parrot, that's all."

"Thanks for that, genius."

"How many boyfriends have you had?"

"One. He lasted...a long time. Way too long." She picks up a forkful of beet salad but doesn't put it in her mouth. "I met Stephen in university, and we lived together for a while. It did not end well. He cheated on me." Her grip tightens on her fork.

Instinctively, I reach across the table and cover her other hand with mine. I'm stroking her fingers before I realize what I'm doing.

"Is this okay?" I ask.

She nods.

"I'll only do it if you like it."

"I do," she whispers, looking down. "It's hard for me to let someone in, but it sounds like it's easy for you. Thirteen relationships? I can't imagine going through that thirteen times."

"Well, none of my relationships ended quite like that. And not all of them were serious."

"But the beginning, I mean. Just opening yourself up."

"I've always liked being in a relationship."

"I liked it, too. At least, I thought I did. Afterward, I wondered how much of it was real, and how deluded I was. Men suck."

I don't argue.

Now I get why Valerie said "no" when I asked her out, even though she seems to be attracted to me. She had a bad experience with her last boyfriend and has trouble trusting men. I don't blame her.

The server puts two plates in front of us. My pancake is crispy and golden brown. It's folded in half and stuffed with stew, and it looks delicious.

I let go of Valerie's hand and use my knife to cut through the pancake. Steam rises. I pick up a bite with my fork and blow on it before popping it in my mouth.

"This is really good," I say.

"Yeah, so is this."

"Want to try some?"

When she nods eagerly, I chuckle and deposit a bite onto her plate.

"It's good," she agrees, "but mine is even more *scrumdiddlyumptious*."

She lets me try some of hers, and oh, she might be right. That's some quality bulgogi. But I don't admit that I might like hers more than my own; I'm just happy she's enjoying herself. And pleased with myself for picking this restaurant.

After dinner, we amble down the street. I'm not ready for this date to end.

"Let's do something naughty," I say with a mischievous smile.

So many wonderful scenes float through my mind, all of them involving Valerie in various states of undress.

But that's not what I'm going to suggest.

"Let's eat ice cream at a place that isn't Ginger Scoops," I say. "There's a Thai rolled ice cream place in Kensington Market."

We stroll west on Baldwin Street. It's a nice night. Warmish, but with a cool breeze. I shove my hands in my pockets so I'm not tempted to hold her hand.

Well, that's not quite true. I'm still tempted, but at least now I've put a little distance between me and temptation.

We soon reach the ice cream shop, which could best be described as *Instagrammable*. It's a simple space with a light purple wall behind the area where the workers stir-fry ice cream. The counter looks like marble. At the front of the shop are a few tables and chairs of light-colored wood, and there are two square shelves at chest level for taking pretty pictures of your ice cream, as one woman is doing now.

Valerie rolls her eyes.

On the wall behind the cash register, there's a list of six choices. Each one includes an ice cream flavor plus toppings.

"What do you want?" she asks. "Probably best if we share. They look big."

Not gonna lie, I like the idea of sharing ice cream with her. Very date-like.

"Why don't you pick?" I say.

"No, you're the one who wanted to come here."

"Since I picked the ice cream spot, you should pick the ice cream."

"Fine," she says.

"You sound awfully pissy about getting what you want."

"It's an impossible decision. I don't want to make it."

"Which ones are you deciding between?"

"All of them!"

I chuckle.

"What?" she demands.

"You're cute."

She gives me a glare that isn't quite as icy as I suspect she thinks it is.

"How about this?" I say. "I'll pick two, and you can decide between them. That okay?"

She agrees.

It really is a tough decision, but I eventually pick Thai iced tea and chocolate-strawberry. The first has Thai tea-flavored ice cream rolls, which are garnished with whipped cream plus a small waffle cone and drizzled with condensed milk; the second contains strawberry ice cream rolls garnished with whipped cream, chocolate shavings, chocolate sauce, fresh strawberries, and chocolate Pocky.

I'm kind of hoping she chooses the chocolate-strawberry, as I think it will make a more exciting Instagram picture, and yeah, I'm totally planning on putting this on Instagram. To needle her, if nothing else.

"I don't know," she says. "They both sound good."

"Alright, let's flip a coin." I pull out a quarter. "Which one's heads?"

"Thai iced tea."

I throw the coin in the air, catch it, and slap it on the back of my hand.

It's heads.

"Thai iced tea it is," I say.

"Okay."

"Is it just my imagination, or are you a little disappointed?"

She worries her bottom lip between her teeth, and I refrain from telling her again that she's cute. "Um... No. It's good."

"I think you're disappointed."

"Okay, fine. You win." She throws up her hands. "The coin toss made me realize I'd prefer the chocolate-strawberry, but it seems so excessive. Chocolate shavings *and* chocolate sauce? It's like when kids get sundaes at Ginger Scoops and decide they want literally everything on them. Also, strawberries and chocolate seem, well...romantic."

"Lucky for you, we're on a date."

She narrows her eyes.

"I hereby decree," I say, "that strawberries and chocolate are an entirely unromantic combination, even if we're sharing. Will you have it now?"

"Too bad they don't have a durian one. I'd definitely get that."

"I know. And I'd get my own chocolate-strawberry and eat it as far away from you as possible. But really, we should have the one you want the most, even if you think it's excessive."

At last she nods her assent, and I go up to the counter and pay for our ice cream. Then we watch as a woman pours some white liquid onto a cold metal surface, covers it with a few squeezes of red sauce and "stir fries" it with a metal spatula. When it's all frozen and spread out in a thin layer, she uses the spatula to roll it into six pink cylinders, each containing several thin layers of the frozen dessert. These are placed in a purple disposable cup with a white rose logo. Next, she adds the garnishes before placing the cup on the counter for us. I grab it before Valerie can and bring it to one of the shelves for a picture.

"Are you serious?" Valerie asks. "You're one of those people?"

I don't take pictures of my food all that often, but I do on occasion, and I'm definitely going to do it to annoy her now.

I snap a few photos. "Hmm. I think I need to play with the settings."

"That's enough!" Valerie grabs the ice cream off its perch and takes it to a table by the window. "It's going to melt if you keep that up."

I chuckle as I sit down across from her, then help myself to one of the Pocky before trying the ice cream. I get a bite with a generous amount of chocolate sauce; Valerie's first bite, in contrast, is about half ice cream and half whipped cream.

"You glad we got the chocolate-strawberry?" I ask.

"Yeah," she says, as though it's painful for her to admit. "I love chocolate."

"More or less than you love durian?"

"Good question." She has some more ice cream, and I watch as she slides the white plastic spoon into her mouth, jealous of it for getting to touch her lips and tongue.

Yeah, that's right, I'm jealous of a plastic spoon.

This may be a new low, but I'm on a (fake) date with a pretty girl and we've eaten lots of delicious food. So my life really isn't too bad.

"I prefer durian," she says.

I gasp and put my hand to my mouth. "How dare you slander chocolate like that! What did chocolate ever do to you?"

She shakes her head. "Sometimes you're kind of annoying, you know."

"Who, me?"

It's so much fun to get under her nerves, and I want to kiss that scowl off her face. She's forcing the scowl—I can see a smile trying to break through.

I take my spoon and scoop up some ice cream, strawberry pieces, and chocolate shavings, and I bring it to her lips. "For you," I whisper. "Indulge me."

She holds my gaze, her wide dark eyes focused on mine. She has such lovely eyes, framed by lovely eyelashes. And then she leans forward and slides the ice cream off the spoon with her lips, and I feel victorious.

It's a strange thing, feeding someone like this. We're not touching, but it's very intimate nonetheless. She's still staring at my eyes, and after she swallows, she parts her lips, and I can see a shudder pass through her.

"Too cold?" I murmur.

"Yes. Too cold."

Liar. I don't say that, though. I won't win Valerie over by calling her out on her reaction to me. But we had a good time tonight, and I'm patient.

We walk back to Yonge Street. I offer to drive her home, but she says she'll take transit.

"Text me when you get there," I tell her outside College Park.

She kisses me on the cheek.

And then she's gone, and my skin prickles where it touched her lips.

Chapter 7

Valerie

A HORRIFYING THING HAPPENS on Wednesday: I start humming to myself.

Humming.

I'm not joking.

During my break in the afternoon, I head to Moonbeam Messages, the small greeting card and gift shop a few doors down from Happy as Pie. I casually peruse the rack of cards, picking up a few here and there. I skip over the birthday cards in favor of the small selection of romantic cards, the kind you'd get for your significant other just because.

One card has two smiling cartoon limes and the line, "You're My Main Squeeze."

Another has two cashews and says, "I'm Nuts for You."

It's when I'm looking at a "Two Hearts Together Forever" card that I realize I'm humming "Something About the Way You Look Tonight."

Hmph.

I immediately stop humming and continue with my important mission: find a card for Peter to give to me. I figure if my mom sees a card in my room, it'll be good evidence of our relationship, and it gives me an excuse to go to this cutesy store that I'd never admit to liking.

There's a small selection of kirigami pop-up cards with no text inside, and I select one with a series of hearts in decreasing size. Better to get this than something corny, like "I'm nuts for you."

But to my dismay, I *am* a little nuts for him. There's no denying that. We had a good time together on Sunday, and I feel like I can let down my guard with him.

Yeah, Peter is an awesome boyfriend.

Fake boyfriend.

I have to keep reminding myself of that.

After purchasing the card, I return to Ginger Scoops and serve ice cream. Chloe is in the back, making strawberry-lychee sorbet.

A single man comes in, and I immediately freeze. He's probably ten years older than me. White. Wedding ring, but as I've learned, that doesn't matter.

I usually try to smile at customers, something that doesn't come naturally to me, but when it's a single man or group of men, I don't.

Because sometimes men interpret a friendly customer service smile as me being interested in them. It's only happened a few times, but those times stick out in my mind, and such men also suck at taking no for an answer.

So I do my best to look unattractive and unfriendly.

Men can accuse you of leading them on even if you do absolutely nothing to encourage it, as I've unfortunately learned.

"Hello," I say to the guy on the other side of the counter. "What can I get you today?"

"I hear you make an excellent green tea ice cream."

"We do."

"Can I try a sample?"

I hand him a plastic spoon with the requested ice cream.

"Mm," he says. "That's good." Then he looks at me in a way that makes my skin prickle unpleasantly.

I'm unnerved. I want him to get out of here as fast as possible.

"You know," he says, "you would be very pretty if you smiled."

Dear God, he's one of *those* men.

"Come on, it's a beautiful day, isn't it?"

"It is," I say tersely.

He probably thinks I'm a frigid bitch, but I don't give a shit. At least when I'm at Ginger Scoops, with its big windows at the front and Chloe in the back room, I do feel safe.

Just very uncomfortable.

It's been drilled into me to not make a scene, plus I don't want Chloe getting bad reviews on her business because of me. So, like the last time this happened, I refuse to smile, but I don't lay into him like I want to. I don't tell him that it's fucking bullshit for men to expect women to smile, like we're just there to amuse them and make their day pleasant.

"Would you like a scoop of green tea ice cream in a cup?" I ask. "A cone? Is there anything else you want to try?"

The asshole looks like he wants to make more annoying comments, but fortunately, the only words out of his mouth are, "A sugar cone."

I scoop out the ice cream for him, and once he heads out the door, I exhale.

Because of #metoo, some men are complaining that every interaction with a woman freaks them out, and they're afraid of being alone with a woman because she might accuse them of sexual assault.

I have no patience for those men.

They complain that one false accusation might torpedo their career, when so many men are given the benefit of the doubt over and over again, whereas one true accusation of sexual harassment literally cost me my career, and now I'm just another STEM woman who no longer works in STEM.

I exhale slowly.

As if she has some kind of sixth sense, Chloe comes out of the back room.

"What's wrong?" she asks.

I just shake my head, but the great thing about knowing someone for many years is that you don't always need words to communicate.

Nobody else is in Ginger Scoops, and she wraps her arms around me. I rest my head on her shoulder for a moment, and I feel a little better.

After work, I meet up with Peter again. His idea this time.

I feel like we're taking this fake relationship more seriously than necessary, but it's nice having something to do with my time, and I can tell my mother, without needing to lie, that I was with Peter.

We meet at a nearby independent coffee shop, one that's open late. I order tea, and they give me a little teapot with loose tea leaves. I can't believe the sight of the mini teapot excites me, but it does.

I try not to show my excitement to Peter as I take my pot of jasmine tea over to the table. He, thankfully, doesn't bother taking a picture for Instagram.

We chat about the weather and other inane things, and then he says, "Do you like working in an ice cream shop?"

"Not really." I'm surprised by my honesty. It's been a long, crappy day, I guess. "But it is what it is. Chloe treats me well."

"What did you do before Ginger Scoops?"

"I was a software developer. I have a degree in computer science."

"You didn't want to do that anymore?"

"I…" I shake my head. "Never mind."

"What?" He's not being pushy. He's kind.

That kindness undoes me.

What the fuck is wrong with me?

All of a sudden, tears prick at the back of my eyes, and God, isn't this just great. I'm going to cry at a coffee shop with my fake boyfriend.

"I couldn't do it anymore. I just couldn't." I swallow as a few tears slide down my cheeks. I still want to drink my tea, but I don't want to sit here any longer. I get up, knocking the table in the process, and my mug almost topples to the ground, but Peter catches it.

"You want to go?" He hands me a napkin.

He's so fucking nice and respectful. I'm not used to this. My family is just loud, and I feel like I'm always fighting back.

"I can get to-go cups for us," he says.

"Okay."

Five minutes later, I'm walking down Dundas with my tea in my hand. It's not unpleasant outside, but there's a bit of a brisk wind. Peter puts his arm around me.

"How about we go back to my place?" he suggests. "It's not far from here. Nothing will happen, I promise. Just for half an hour, and then I can drive you home."

"Oh, you don't have to do that."

"I don't have to be your fake boyfriend, but here we are."

I snicker at that. "Okay, sounds good."

His place is a one-bedroom in a glass building that's maybe ten years old. It's not immaculate, but it's reasonably clean, decorated mostly in grays and blues. It's a bit cluttered, but that's understandable, as it's pretty small as far as one-bedrooms go.

And now I'm jealous.

"I've never lived alone," I tell him as he gestures for me to sit at the kitchen table.

He pulls out a blue cookie tin, the kind that's usually filled with sewing supplies in my family, but this one actually contains butter cookies. I reach for one.

"It's nice being away from people," I say. "Ginger Scoops was busy all day, and now I finally feel like I can breathe. I liked sitting behind a computer in my cubicle all day. I miss that."

"I'd hate to work in an office," Peter says.

"How long have you done landscaping?"

"Since I finished university. I used to plant trees up north in the summers, and I always enjoyed that."

"That's really hard work, isn't it? Did you get paid by the tree?"

He nods.

"I wouldn't have lasted a day," I say.

"I'm sure you would have." He pauses. "Do you want to do software development again? You said you couldn't, but do you *want* to?"

I don't reply but change the topic. "I'd love to live alone. Living with my family is, well, chaotic. But it's expensive to have your own place, and I don't make a lot of money. One day, maybe."

I don't let myself think about the future too much, because whenever I do, I get sad. Instead, I focus on getting through each day, putting one foot in front of the other. I can't think about how everything blew up in my face; I just have to make sure I'm never in that position again.

Yet despite all the ways men have screwed me over in my personal life and my career, I'm still here. Alone. With Peter. And this isn't for show.

Maybe I shouldn't trust him at all. Maybe he's an asshole deep inside. Nice men often turn out to be complete assholes.

But I can't help it. I like being here with him.

We eat cookies and drink our tea in silence for a few minutes. I take a moment to admire Peter, the light and shadows playing across his face. He really is handsome, even more so than I initially thought. His hair is a touch long, but I like it on him, and he has that goddamn smile that just seems...peaceful. Content. Like he's okay with the way everything is going in his life, even though he's sitting in his kitchen at ten thirty at night with a fake girlfriend who started crying in a coffee shop.

He inches his hand across the table and places it on top of mine.

"I should go home," I say. "It's getting late."

"Will you let me drive you today?"

Half an hour later, we're pulling into my driveway.

The thought of being separated from Peter feels oddly unnerving. I don't want this to end, yet I'm embarrassed that he's already seen me cry. Stephen and I had been together for over a year by the time he finally saw me shed tears.

I'm embarrassed, but less embarrassed than I would have expected. Strange.

Peter leans over, as if to kiss me, but then pulls back. "Goodnight."

"Goodnight," I say, then head inside.

I'm just slipping off my shoes when I realize that I forgot to give Peter the card.

Oh, well. Next time.

To my surprise, my parents are already in bed, and Sabrina is in her bedroom, likely studying. Nobody bothers me as I go to my own room, shut the door, and lean against it, unable to calm the strange feelings that have been stirred up inside me.

Chapter 8

Peter

I'm sitting on the patio at Ginger Scoops, waiting for Valerie's mother and trying to think of some cool embellishments for my story. Maybe I once saved a child from a burning building and the mayor presented me with an award.

Nah, better make it three children. That's more impressive.

Maybe I graduated at the top of my class in med school.

I chuckle at the thought. I wasn't a particularly strong math and science student. I mean, I wasn't terrible, but I wasn't great, and my parents always reassured me with their "we all have our own strengths and special gifts!" talk.

I suppose I'm thankful for that.

Hmm. Maybe in addition to being a doctor, I'm a champion ping pong player or golfer or figure skater.

Maybe I only need two hours of sleep a night and spend my free time learning languages.

Maybe I was a music prodigy and became a concert pianist at the age of eight.

Maybe I won a national spelling bee.

My phone buzzes and I look at the screen.

DAD: We went to Hanlan's Point today. Thought I'd send you some pictures.

I yelp. No, I do not want to see pictures from my parents' trip to a clothing-optional beach, thank you very much.

"Peter? What's wrong?"

I look up and see a woman of about sixty frowning at me.

Well, that's great timing.

I jump to my feet. "Hi, Mrs. Chow. It's great to meet you. Just got some bad news about the test results for a patient, that's all," I say breezily.

"Ah, call me Cynthia," she says. "Your job must be stressful, yes?"

I nod. "Stressful, long hours, but I wouldn't trade it for anything." I pause. "Would you like some ice cream?"

"No, that's okay."

I'm not sure how to do this. I've met a girlfriend's mother many times before, but never have I met a girlfriend's mother while lying about being a pediatrician. Never have I met a girlfriend's mother at an ice cream shop.

My cellphone buzzes again. Probably pictures from a nudist beach.

I don't look.

"You should get that," Cynthia says. "I know you're an important man. Maybe it's more test results."

Now I feel like I have to get it, but I make sure she can't see the screen.

There's a picture of the Toronto skyline, as viewed from the Toronto Islands. No people in sight. I breathe out a sigh of relief.

"My parents," I say. "I'll talk to them later."

"What do your parents do?" she asks.

"My dad's retired. He used to work at Fong Investments."

She nods her approval.

"My mother..."

Oh, dear.

I'm tempted to lie. Tempted to tell Cynthia that my mother is a pharmacist, optometrist, engineer, or similar.

But even though I was thinking up lies I could tell about myself earlier, I figure it's best if I stick to the truth here.

"My mother is an artist."

"Would I know any of her work?"

"I doubt it."

This, I'm aware, is not quite meeting Cynthia's approval, but more details aren't going to help. *My mother's paintings celebrate women's sexuality. She had an installation at Nuit Blanche last year, and she used to work as an art therapist.*

I once gave that description to a former girlfriend's parents, and it did not go over well, especially when they insisted on seeing some of her work. They assumed I was lying about the "celebrating women's sexuality" part.

I was not lying.

I'm not ashamed of my mother, but life would be easier if she had a different occupation.

"Your last name?" Cynthia says.

Right. I know Valerie has refrained from mentioning it so far because she doesn't want her family to google me, but if I refuse to give my last name, it will seem suspicious.

"It's So," I say, not wanting to lie about that, either.

"And your parents are from Hong Kong?"

"Yes, but they were both raised in Canada."

Her eyebrows shoot up. "Do you speak Cantonese at all?"

"Not much."

She clucks her tongue. I wonder what she'd say if she knew what I actually do for work.

"Are you sure I can't get you something?" I ask. "If not ice cream, then tea or coffee?"

"Coffee would be nice, yes. Valerie knows how I like it."

I head inside to get us each a coffee, rather glad to have a break from that conversation.

"One coffee for me and one for your mother," I say to Valerie.

"How's it going?" she asks.

"Not bad, but I told her that my mom paints pictures of vaginas."

"Peter!"

"What? It's the truth." I grin. "Just kidding. I kept it at 'artist,' don't worry."

When I return to the patio and hand Cynthia her coffee, she returns to questioning me. "Where did you go to med school?"

"U of T."

"And for undergrad?"

"Queen's."

She nods. "What made you decide to be a pediatrician?"

"I really like children."

Which is true. At least, I like most children. My cousin has twins who are absolute terrors, and I can't say I particularly enjoy it when they're around. I'm not sure how my cousin doesn't have severe hearing loss by now, because...wow.

But in general? Kids are good.

"So, you want to have children of your own?" Cynthia asks.

"I do."

"Tell me, which hospital are you at right now?"

"SickKids."

"What rotation are you doing?"

Unfortunately, I have no idea how medical residencies work. Nobody in my family is a doctor, nor are any of my friends, and it was never of interest to me. But apparently there are rotations?

"Um," I say. "Broken bones."

That's one of the main reasons children would have to go to the hospital, isn't it?

Cynthia looks at me like I have two heads.

Right. I might have broken a couple of bones when I was younger, but that doesn't sound like a proper medical rotation.

"Just kidding," I say, although why I'd be kidding about something like this, I don't know. "I'm doing a rotation in the ICU."

"The NICU or the PICU?"

"NICU." That's the one with babies, right?

I'm making a hash of this.

I'm usually better at the meet-the-parents business, but it's tough when I'm supposed to pretend I'm something I'm not.

"Valerie had to be in the NICU for a month after she was born," Cynthia says, her voice suddenly quiet. "She came early, so tiny. We were very worried. But they treat us well, here in Canada. I just didn't always understand what the doctors were telling me, you know? Because my English wasn't perfect then, and I didn't know all the fancy medical words. That's why it would be good for Valerie to marry a doctor—if anything happens, you will be able to understand it all. Be in a good position to make decisions." She looks off into the distance, and I get the feeling she hasn't talked about this in a long time. "Everything turned out okay, though. I just want her to be a smart, successful woman."

"And she is."

Cynthia grunts. "She's not reaching her full potential, but hopefully you will help her do that."

What does Cynthia see as Valerie's "full potential"? I assume this is related to Valerie's previous career. I have no idea what happened, but I do know it's a sore spot.

"Valerie is perfect the way she is," I say, needing to defend her.

Cynthia smiles. "You really like her."

"Of course."

"Good, good."

Valerie walks toward us. "Are you scaring him off, Mom?"

"Me?" Cynthia's voice is upbeat again. "Of course not! He tells me he is working in the NICU right now—why would I want to scare him off? You should marry this one."

I guess I didn't make too much of a hash of this. Turns out I said exactly what she wanted to hear.

"But if you're not careful," Cynthia continues, "someone else will snap him up. You must keep him happy."

"You're talking about me as though I'm a piece of meat," Valerie says.

"Wah, not a piece of meat! Well, maybe a very expensive, delicious cut of meat."

I snicker. I can't help it.

"Clearly you were not keeping Stephen happy!"

Valerie balls her hands into fists. "Stop it. Don't you dare talk about Stephen."

"Fine, fine. Just saying, that's all." Cynthia stands up and turns to me. "I hope the test results for your patient are not as bad as they seem."

"What patient?" Valerie asks.

"Oh, one of the babies in the NICU," I say airily.

I better make sure my lies don't get out of control.

Valerie brings me a double scoop of taro and matcha cheesecake ice cream in a bubble waffle, along with an envelope.

Careful not to spill any ice cream on it, I open up the envelope and find a blank card with an elaborate set of pop-up red hearts inside.

My heart kicks up a notch. She got me a card! And it's such a cute one. I've never seen a pop-up card quite like this before.

"You forgot something," I tell her. "You didn't sign it."

"Ah, sorry. The card isn't for you."

"Huh?"

"It's for you to give to me. So just sign your name and draw a few hearts or something and give it back to me. I'll put it in my bedroom, my mother will see it, and it will fit our act."

"What should I write?" I lean back in my chair and lick the taro ice cream. It's good, but not as good as the matcha cheesecake. I'm particularly fond of that one because it reminds me of when Valerie and I had Japanese cheesecake. "Maybe, 'Valerie, darling, you are the light of my life'?"

She mimes throwing up.

"What about, 'Roses are red, violets are blue, sugar is sweet, and durian is disgusting'?"

"That doesn't rhyme."

"Is that your only objection?"

"You know I object to calling durian 'disgusting.'"

"When did you first try it?"

"I was nine, I think. My mother has some family in Malaysia, and we went for two weeks when her cousin got married." There's a dreamy smile on her face, which makes me smile, too. "I remember running on the beach with my cousins...the hot weather...the durian. It was a nice trip."

"Valerie," I say, "if you want me to give you a card, just tell me. I can pick it out myself." I lick my matcha cheesecake ice cream, and her gaze seems to be fixated on my tongue.

Excellent.

"I'll keep that in mind for next time," she says, "but for now, you can give me this card."

I think for a moment, then write something simple: *The last few weeks with you have been amazing, and I look forward to more time with you.* I hand the card back to Valerie.

"Thank you for not including any bad poetry about durian," she says.

"You're welcome."

"How did it go with my mom?"

I shrug. "I told her that my current rotation is in, uh, broken bones, before changing it to the NICU. She approved. She wants me to help you reach your full potential."

Valerie rolls her eyes. "Yeah, she doesn't approve of this." She gestures around the patio. "But at least I have a hot doctor as a boyfriend now, so she has something to like. Just don't say anything stupid, okay?"

"I solemnly swear to do my best."

She touches my knee, just for a moment, before she heads inside.

The truth is, I could write lots of poetry about durian, hopefully better than the line I came up with earlier.

You see, I think Valerie is like a durian.

Now hear me out. I'm not saying she's spiky and stinky. In fact, she smells vaguely of vanilla and coconut—I like her scent. Though she's kind of spiky on the outside, it's true.

Inside, however, she's a bit mushy. Sensitive.

I like her contradictions.

I don't know everything that happened to her, but I want to know. She told me it's hard for her to let someone in, and I feel like she *is* letting me in, slowly, and I don't think anything good will come from trying to push her too fast. She let someone in once, and he screwed her over; I suspect she was always hesitant and wary, but even more so now than she was before. I hate him for hurting her.

I just want to be the guy she tells things to. The guy who knows everything about her. I want to get further past the spikes than I have so far.

To Valerie, durian is a delicious treat that not everyone appreciates.

I see her the way she sees durian.

Chapter 9

Valerie

IT'S ONE IN THE morning. My father is asleep. My sister is asleep.

My mother is still out playing mahjong.

I sigh and open the kirigami heart card again. *The last few weeks with you have been amazing, and I look forward to more time with you.*

I've read those words over and over. I'm glad he wrote something sweet but not mawkish.

But it's not real.

I told Peter to write me a card, and he did. He's just playing his part.

Still, whenever I read it, a frisson of heat runs through me. I think of him casually chatting with my mother on the patio, not having a clue what he was talking about when it came to medicine, yet not freaking out.

I admire people like Peter. People who go with the flow, who never get too worked up about anything.

Unlike me.

I sip my tea, then put the card aside and return to my novel. If I'm honest with myself, I rather like it when my mom goes out late because it's the only time I get any real solitude. It's the only time I can hear myself think.

Tonight, I'm thinking that I like Peter, I really do, even if this is supposed to be fake.

Before I lose my nerve, I send him a text. *Hey, you want to hang out tomorrow evening?*

To my surprise, he replies right away.

We start at Pupusa Hut, an El Salvadoran restaurant on Baldwin Street. It's crowded, bustling with people who are here for a late meal or snack. We place our orders before grabbing the last available high-top by the door.

Peter's knee bumps against mine under the table, and it causes the same response in me as reading over the greeting card. There's just something about his smile and his touch—even an accidental banging of knees—that hits me in the chest. I can't stay away.

"What did you do at work today?" I ask. "Leaf raking? Hedge trimming?"

"There's this rich guy on the Bridle Path—the durian guy, actually—who pays us to maintain the hedge maze in his backyard."

"He has his own hedge maze? That seems extravagant. Does he hide durians in it?"

"Thankfully, no. That would be an unpleasant surprise. I did, however, find evidence that his latest orgy made its way to the maze."

The tips of my ears heat. "Orgy?"

"That's the rumor, and after finding two bras in the maze today, I suspect it's true."

"Bras are expensive. I would never leave one in a hedge."

He chuckles. "If you were rich, would you hire someone to make a hedge maze in your backyard?"

"No, I'd use my money for other things."

"Like what? Million-dollar fountains or birdbaths? Would you commission someone to make a sculpture of you? A large oil painting?"

"Why would I want a sculpture of myself?"

He shrugs. "Vanity?"

"I'm not that vain."

"You should be. You're very pretty, even when you scowl like that."

"I'm not scowling."

"Yes, you are." He reaches out and trails his finger over my cheek. "So, what would you do if you were filthy rich?"

"I'd save most of it. You never know when everything you have could go up in flames." I pause. "And I'd buy a house so I could have my own space. Maybe a house with a really tall hedge around the yard."

"Ah. A tall hedge to provide cover for your durian orgies. Of course. It's only sensible."

I shoot him a glare. "I'm not having durian orgies!"

Just then, a server sets our food in front of us.

It's not just the tips of my ears that are turning pink now. My whole face is on fire, and I'm unable to speak.

Peter, however, has no such trouble. "Thank you very much," he says to the server. "This looks delicious."

We ordered four pupusas. The thick corn tortillas are stuffed with beans, meat, and cheese, and they're accompanied by cabbage slaw. It's all delicious.

We eat in silence, and I'm glad to focus on my food for a few minutes, although it's not like I can forget about Peter sitting across from me.

"What would you like to do next?" he asks before he digs into his second pupusa. "I have a couple of ideas. Karaoke?"

"No goddamn way am I doing karaoke."

"That's fine. We don't have to do anything else. I can walk you to the subway afterward. Just thought I'd ask."

"Let's do something. But not karaoke."

The corner of his mouth kicks up. He's wearing a dark blue polo shirt today, and he looks incredibly handsome...and I'm not willing to let him go just yet.

"Alright," he says. "There's a bar on Queen Street, not far from here. They serve desserts from the bakery next door, including an awesome flourless chocolate cake. On Friday nights, there's a live brass band, and people get up to dance. It's lots of fun."

"You want to take me *dancing*?" I ask in horror.

He grins. "Yeah."

"So my choices are karaoke and dancing."

"Hey, you're welcome to suggest something else. Those are just my ideas, and you're the one who wanted to hang out tonight." He has a bite of his pupusa and leans forward. "Is this a real date, Valerie?"

"I...I don't know. I just wanted to see you."

"Come dancing with me."

"I can't dance."

"I'm sure you can. No fancy moves required. Why don't we go and have the cake, and then you can decide?"

"Okay."

He places his hand over mine. "I wanted to see you tonight, too."

My heart beats way too quickly.

Half an hour later, we're sitting at a table in the bar, a slice of flourless chocolate cake between us, and oh my God, Peter is right. This is amazing.

When I first heard of flourless chocolate cake a few years ago, I was confused. I thought flour was an essential part of cake. But then I discovered that it's richer and more chocolatey without flour, and this is the best version I've ever had. I moan in bliss. I doubt anyone can hear me because we're sitting near the brass band and the music is a little loud. There's a small crowd of people dancing in front of us.

"You know what?" I say. "This is even better than durian."

He smiles at me. "Glad to hear you've developed normal taste buds."

The lights in the bar are dim. There are mismatched wooden chairs and tables, each with a little candle in the middle. The candlelight flickers over Peter's face, and he smiles.

I have a sip of my red wine before taking another bite of chocolate cake.

"I need to eat quickly," Peter says, "or I won't get my share."

"Wait a second," I say. "You have to eat quickly because *I'm* eating quickly? I'm only eating this fast because I was worried I wouldn't get my share because *you're* practically inhaling the cake."

"No, no. You're the reason we're eating so fast."

"Am not!"

He laughs and cuts the remainder of the slice of cake in half. "Yours and mine. Now we can eat as slowly as we like."

He picks up a forkful of cake and slides it into his mouth.

"Mmmmm," he says in an exaggerated fashion.

Or maybe it isn't exaggerated. The cake really is delicious.

Once we're finished eating, Peter takes my hand. "Time to dance?"

I finish my wine. "Time to dance."

I could say no, of course. Peter would listen. But even as my mind resists the idea of dancing—as always—a part of me wants to dance, as long as it's with him. And he seems to be able to tell when I secretly want to do something versus when I absolutely do not—like karaoke.

He leads me to the dance floor. I put one hand on his shoulder, and he puts his on my waist; I feel the heat of his touch through my shirt. He holds my other hand in his.

"This okay?" he asks.

I nod, overwhelmed by his closeness, his firm body nearly touching mine.

He rocks us back and forth a few times, then spins me around. For a brief moment, it's like I'm flying, and just when I'm starting to feel out of control, he pulls me back toward him, and I laugh.

We continue to dance, not precisely in time with the music. Peter might not have sophisticated moves on the dance floor, but he's better than me, and what he lacks in skill, he makes up for in enthusiasm. He's taking me along for the ride, and I love it.

I laugh again, for no particular reason, and he smiles.

The dance floor won't clear so everyone can watch our amazing moves. We're just part of the crowd, and that's what I want. I don't want everyone looking at me. I only want to dance with Peter, feeling like we're in our own little world, even though we're surrounded by people.

I've never enjoyed dancing before. I may have agreed to the occasional slow dance and shuffled my feet back and forth, but I would never dance a fast song like this with a man. My fears and self-consciousness would have paralyzed me.

But all I have to do is follow Peter's lead, and I feel...safe. Which is a strange emotion to have while dancing in a bar to a brass band, but there it is.

I'm disappointed when the band takes a break. We separate and return to our seats. Tentatively, I slide my hand across the table, and Peter covers it with his.

"I have to tell you something," he says. "I feel guilty for keeping it a secret."

My stomach drops.

Crap, this is it. I've had a great night with a guy and now he's going to reveal he's married or runs a dog-fighting ring or—

"I agreed to the fake relationship mostly because I was hoping you'd eventually change your mind and agree to date me for real. I should have told you that upfront. I'm sorry."

Oh.

I see the look on his face, and I remember what it was like to dance in his arms, and I know it's true. He wants me, very much, even now that we've gotten to know each other, even though I've been difficult at times.

"That's okay," I say, swallowing hard. "You asked me out when we first met, so the fact that you want to...you know." I gesture between us. "That's not exactly a surprise."

A part of me feels like I knew it all along, and I was just trying not to think of it because I'd sworn off relationships.

I remember all three men who fucked up my life last year, and I pull my hand back.

"I don't know what I want," I say.

"Just let me take you out occasionally. Like tonight. No expectations. I'd like to keep seeing you, and not just as part of our act."

"It's hard for me to trust men."

"I only want a chance to earn that trust. We'll never do anything you don't want, and I promise I won't keep anything else from you, okay?"

How is he so understanding? Does he really not have any ulterior motives?

I blow out a breath. "Okay. Thank you. I'm sorry, I'm kind of broken."

"Not broken," he says firmly. "And I'm sure there's a good reason for what you're feeling. You don't owe me anything. I'd just like the opportunity to do this again."

I nod. "And I'd like the opportunity to eat another piece of flourless chocolate cake. Right now."

He laughs and asks the waitress for more cake. It's not long before there's a second piece on our table, and this time, Peter cuts it down the middle before anyone takes a bite.

I turn the plate around and claim the slice that was initially on his side.

"What was wrong with the other slice?" he asks.

"This one's bigger."

"Why do you get the bigger one?"

"You cut, so I get to pick. That's just the way it works."

"Is it, now?"

"Mm-hmm," I say around a mouthful of the best damn chocolate cake I've ever tasted.

If I ate it without Peter, would it taste this good?

I think so, but I can't be sure.

The band starts playing again, and once we finish our cake, I pull Peter onto the dance floor. I attempt to spin him around with one hand, but he's several inches taller than me, and it doesn't work very well. We laugh together, and then he pulls my back against his chest, and we dance like that for a while. I can feel his breath on my cheek; I can smell chocolate on his breath.

It's a lovely combination.

And, once again, I feel safe when he holds me. I remind myself not to let my guard down, but I do feel safe in his arms.

He dips his head. "You look beautiful tonight."

My instinct is to object. I'm wearing the jeans and T-shirt I wore to work today.

But I swallow my protests. I should learn to accept compliments.

"You look good, too," I whisper.

His eyes crinkle and the corner of his mouth curls up, sending a bolt of heat straight to my core. Damnit, he's so sexy. And he's dancing. With me.

We dance for another half hour, and I'm only distantly aware of the crowd around us. It's just me and Peter. He's so solid against me, and I run my hand up and down his upper arm muscles, appreciating every inch of his body. In awe of him, and the fact that we're together like this.

When my fingers skate over his shoulder and graze his neck, he says, "Let's get out of here."

He pays the bill, and then he pulls me out the door and down the nearby Graffiti Alley. He doesn't push me up against the spray-painted wall, but gently guides me to it and places his hands on my waist.

I look into his dark eyes. I swear, I could drown in them, and then I laugh.

"What is it?" he asks with a slight smile.

I shake my head. *Never mind, I'm just having some super embarrassing thoughts.*

He reaches up and pushes a lock of hair back from my face. I'm sweaty from all the dancing, but I know he won't mind.

Somehow, no matter what I do, it's all fine with him.

He tips his forehead against mine. "I had a really good time tonight."

"Me, too," I say, my voice full of eagerness that I've never heard in it before.

Laughter and conversations reach us on the breeze. It's after midnight, but we're in downtown Toronto and there are lots of people out.

"I want to kiss you," he says, "but if you're not ready, that's totally fine. I'll only do it if you tell me to."

Heat washes over my skin.

"Kiss me," I whisper, the anticipation almost more than I can bear.

He starts by pressing his body against mine. With one hand he cups my jaw, his fingers warm and slightly callused. He wraps his other arm around my waist so I'm surrounded by him.

And then he kisses the top of my neck, and oh God, that's good, but I'm impatient. I want his lips on mine. I want to be able to kiss him back.

He makes his way up to my mouth, and when his lips touch mine, I jolt. It's unfamiliar, this feeling of being so safe and turned on at the same time.

"Good?" he murmurs.

"Mm-hmm."

He squeezes my ass in a slow, filthy way that feels so damn good. He pulls me against him, against the ridge of his erection, and I gasp as I try to get closer, need pooling between my thighs.

When he slides both hands under my ass, I wrap both legs around his hips, my back against the wall, and attempt to kiss the shit out of him. I press my breasts against his chest, wanting to touch all of him that I can. He feels so *necessary*.

It's been so long since I've felt this consuming desire, and yet it's okay, as long as it's with him. I shift against his cock, and he growls.

I grin, pleased with the power I have with him.

How can this be happening to me?

If only it were just the two of us, all alone in the world, and he could slide right into me.

But people and traffic are only a few steps away, and it's one thing to make out in an alley, but I wouldn't have sex here. Although I'm much less self-conscious than usual today, that's not something I would do.

And besides the setting, there's everything else.

My past is pushed up against the back corners of my mind, but it's still there. Although this evening with him has loosened something within me, it hasn't loosened everything, and that's okay. It's not a rush.

I lower my feet to the ground, but I keep kissing him. I slide a hand under the cotton of his polo shirt, and his muscles tighten beneath my hands. When I scrape my nails over his skin, he hisses out a breath, and then his hand is under my shirt, his fingers slipping under the edge of my bra. He tweaks my nipple.

"No further...than this." I pant, and he nods.

He continues to fondle my breast as he kisses my collarbone, once again tracing a path upward to my mouth. He gives me an open-mouthed kiss and licks his tongue over my bottom lip before sliding it inside my mouth.

We kiss for a while in a way that's urgent, yet leisurely.

At last, he steps away. "What do you want?"

That's such a complicated question. Different parts of me want different things.

"I want..."

"Yes?"

Peter is breathing hard, and I can see the outline of his erection through his jeans.

But his voice is all patience.

I don't deserve this.

The thought flashes through my brain.

I'm a failed software developer who lives with her parents and works at her friend's ice cream shop even though I loathe customer service.

I invented a boyfriend so my mother would think I'm less of a loser.

My only ex tried to blame his cheating on me, and yes, I know that's ridiculous and he's an asshole, but it's my only experience with a relationship.

Yet here I am.

Even though I'm standing in an alley filled with graffiti, I feel like someone's goddamn princess, a woman who commands the utmost respect.

I wrap my arms around his neck and kiss him once more. "I'd like to go home."

"You want me to drive you? I didn't drink, just a sip of your wine."

"If it's not too much of a hassle..."

"It's no hassle. Are you up for walking back to my place, or should I get an Uber?"

"We can walk."

It's a nice night, but the days are getting ever shorter, and this weather won't last.

On our walk, I do the unthinkable: I hold his hand.

Chapter 10

Valerie

I HEAD UP THE walkway to my parents' house. It's two in the morning, and I can't remember the last time I was out this late. My mother's car is in the driveway.

Finally! I got home later than my mother!

All the lights in the house are out. I open the door and creep up the stairs, trying to make as little noise as possible so I don't wake anyone. I feel like I'm doing something illicit, and it's thrilling.

Of course, there's nothing illicit about eating pupusas and flourless chocolate cake with one's fake boyfriend. Plus, I only had a single glass of wine, and I only made out with said fake boyfriend in an alley for five minutes, but what a great five minutes it was.

I wanted to go to bed with him. My body had come alive in a way I thought it might never do again.

Sex was so tangled up with everything that happened last year, and I had no interest in that mess. Sure, sometimes I still found men attractive. Sometimes I got horny. But I never really felt desire.

Until now.

But that's my body. My head still isn't ready.

Peter makes me feel wonderful, but I have to be very comfortable with someone before I can sleep with them. It's just the way I am, the way it's always been, even more so now than when I was younger.

I brush my teeth and change into a flimsy tank top and shorts. Before I climb into bed, I look at myself in the mirror. At the skin he touched and caressed. My cheeks are slightly flushed and my lips are swollen—or is that my imagination?

I don't know.

I push aside the neckline of my shirt and rub my nipple between my fingers. I tip my head back and exhale unsteadily, remembering what it was like to feel his mouth on mine, his hands all over me. The pleasure he gave me, which I'm sure was only a tiny fraction of what he's capable of.

I breathe in sharply at the thought.

It's been such a long time since I wanted to touch myself.

I crawl under the covers and pull out my vibrator from its special hiding spot. I place it on my pillow, not ready for it quite yet. First, I slip my hand inside my underwear and run my finger over my slit. I'm wet—only a little wet. Stephen always complained that I...

Stop thinking of Stephen!

I rub my clit with my thumb and arch against my hand.

Imagine Peter's hand on you, his fingers on your clit, sliding inside your body...

I don't know what he'd say as he touched me, but I'm sure it would be perfect, because somehow he always knows the right thing to say, and I would melt against him. Surrender to whatever he would give me, knowing it would never be more than I could take. He thinks I should be cherished, but not because I'm made of glass.

I imagine running my hands up his bare arms, over his pecs. Licking a trail down, down his chest, until I reach his boxers and take his cock in my mouth.

This isn't something I've fantasized about before, though I've given a blowjob, of course. But now, the thought of bringing him to orgasm with my mouth is almost unbearably sexy.

I grasp the vibrator and turn it on. It's a quiet one—I got it specifically for that reason. When I press it to my clit, I gasp.

Shit.

Quickly, I cover my mouth with my hand, and then I get to work.

Oh God, it feels so good, but I want more. I want him inside me, I want...

There's a knock on my door.

Oh my fucking God.

Instinctively, I chuck the lime-green vibrator across the room.

Yeah, that was a smart move.

"Valerie?" Mom asks. "What was that noise?"

"Coming!" I say, then snicker.

Jesus, I really need to get it together.

After picking up the vibrator and tossing it in a drawer, I walk to the door and open it a crack.

"It's almost three in the morning," I hiss. "What do you want?"

"Why are you in such a grumpy mood? And what was that thump?" My mother sounds perky despite the late hour.

"Oh, I just dropped my e-reader," I say. "I was reading. A little light reading after my late night out, you know."

"You were with Peter?"

"Yes. With Peter. Yes."

Why am I so bad at this? My heart is thumping wildly in my chest—and not in a good way, like it was earlier.

"Hmm," Mom says, looking at me in a way that makes me shiver. Like she can see right into my brain and knows exactly what I was doing.

Not, of course, that there's anything wrong with a little late-night masturbation after seeing one's fake boyfriend, but this is my freaking mother, and she interrupted me, and I can't help feeling awkward as hell.

"What did you do tonight?" Mom asks.

"Ate dinner, went dancing."

"You went dancing?"

"Shh. You're going to wake everyone up."

"But you hate dancing." She peers at me. "Have you been drinking? Are you on drugs?"

"No, I just felt like dancing. Now, I'm working tomorrow and I'd really like to get some sleep."

Mom regards me suspiciously before leaving my room.

I breathe out a sigh of relief and return to bed, but I don't take out my vibrator. Nope, the mood is ruined.

But after I turn out the lights and cuddle up under the covers, I imagine Peter's arms around me.

"You went *dancing*?" Chloe says. "But you hate dancing!"

"You sound like my mother," I mutter.

It's Sunday night, which is when Chloe, Sarah, and I usually hang out. Both Happy as Pie and Ginger Scoops have shorter hours on Sundays and are closed on Mondays, so none of us have to work tomorrow.

Today, we're at a unicorn bar.

No, I'm not kidding.

We're at a goddamn unicorn bar, which is simply called... Unicorn Bar.

This was not my choice of venue, I assure you. It was Chloe's.

The bar has simple white tables and chairs—I have no objection there. But the servers are all wearing unicorn headbands, there are paintings of unicorns on the walls, and the bar itself looks like it was attacked by rainbows.

Then there are the drinks. Oh, the drinks. They have names like Glitter Bomb, Let's Prance, Magic Dust, and Rainbow Delight.

I tried to order a rum and coke, but Chloe wouldn't let me, so instead I'm drinking a Glitter Bomb. It's a blue cocktail (thanks to blue curacao) with a disturbing amount of edible glitter, and I'm afraid it's going to make me poop rainbows or something.

I have another sip. It's actually quite good, not that I'll admit that to anyone.

"I still can't believe you went dancing." Chloe has a sip of her Rainbow Delight, a layered cocktail with a unicorn pop.

"Well, I did," I say, thinking back to the way Peter spun me around and made me not care about anything except being close to him.

"Oh my God. You have a dopey look on your face!"

"Do not!" I school my features into a perfect frown.

"You do," Sarah says. "Is this relationship not-so-fake after all?"

"It's a fake relationship," I insist. "But, okay, fine, I like him. Happy now?"

"No!" Chloe cries. "You need to tell me more. Are you hoping it will turn into a real relationship?"

"That's what he's hoping."

She bounces in her seat. "Ooh, how exciting!"

"You need to be cut off," I mutter.

"I'm only on my second drink."

"It's not the booze I'm talking about. It's all the goddamn sugar."

"You are such a delight." Chloe throws a unicorn napkin at me.

"I know, that's me. Such a delight. Why couldn't we go to a demon-themed bar instead? Maybe a goth bar where everything was black instead of rainbow-colored?"

"So he hopes it'll turn into a real relationship," Sarah says, "but what do *you* hope?"

"I hope everyone will stop bugging me about my hare-brained idea to have a fake boyfriend."

"But you like him. I know it can be scary—it was scary for me, too, when Josh and I started spending time together, but it's been pretty amazing."

"And Peter got you to go dancing," Chloe says. "This isn't the kind of guy that comes around every day."

"Well, it's not every day you spill durian ice cream on someone."

Chloe places her hand over mine, which is clenched on the table next to the Glitter Bomb. "I think this one might be worth it. You've been happier these past few days."

"I have?" I ask in horror.

She laughs. "Yeah, you've been genuinely smiling, not just customer-service smiling."

"Hmph." I swirl my straw through the glittery blue of my drink. "I guess you're right. Peter is just so...nice. I enjoy being with him."

"Nice" sounds like an empty word, but to me, it's not. It's refreshing to be with someone like that.

Chloe pats my hand. "I'm happy for you. You deserve it, after everything that's happened."

I swallow, uncomfortable, and then something catches my eye. "Do you see what that table ordered? It looks like the ultimate unicorn sundae."

The sundae is large enough for four people. Hell, it would probably feed six or eight. There are several scoops of ice cream in a myriad of colors, topped with an extremely generous amount of whipped cream, fruit, and rainbow sprinkles. There are also six unicorn pops and a unicorn cookie.

I look at my menu. I think that's the Unicorn Deluxe.

This is enough to temporarily distract Chloe from my love life, thank God.

I'm still a bit unsure about the whole Peter thing, though I don't know how to articulate everything I feel. Nor do I feel like sharing the embarrassing my-mother-interrupted-my-masturbation-session story.

But I'm out with my friends and I had a great date on Friday, and life is better than it's been in a while.

It's after midnight when I get home. Sabrina is up, but Mom and Dad are asleep.

I quietly ascend the stairs and get ready for bed, but this time, I do not look at myself in the mirror. I do not take out my vibrator.

I really need to get my own apartment, but it's just so damn expensive. A one-bedroom apartment downtown would cost a lot, and I don't particularly like the idea of having a roommate. I want a place that's all mine. My sanctuary from the world, without any mothers who stay out late playing mahjong and interrupt me at inopportune times.

And without any sisters knocking on my door when I'm about to go to bed.

"I heard a rumor that you went dancing the other night," Sabrina says.

God, why is everyone obsessing about that?

"I did," I say. "Now leave me alone and stop that incessant giggling."

She gives me the finger—in a loving, sisterly way, of course—and I pick up the greeting card on my night table.

I run my finger over Peter's words and smile.

Chapter 11

Peter

I TAP MY FINGERS on the patio table and sip my coffee. I'm at Ginger Scoops, waiting for Valerie to come out and join me for her break. Unfortunately, since it's beautiful weather for the first of October, there are lots of people in line. It'll probably be a little while, but I don't mind waiting if I get to see Valerie.

"Hey. Peter?"

An unfamiliar man takes a seat across from me.

"Yes?" I say warily.

The man is a bit older than me, maybe mid-thirties. East Asian. Wearing a button-down shirt and khakis. Serious-looking. Glasses.

He's completely unfamiliar, and yet he knows my name?

"You're the guy Valerie's seeing," he says.

"Yes?" How does he know that?

"I'm Alan, her brother. I've seen your picture before, that's how I recognized you."

Ah. Okay.

I stick out my hand, but he doesn't shake it. Instead, he looks at me with narrowed eyes.

"Don't fuck around on her," he says. "Or I will come for you."

I try to contain my laughter, but I don't quite manage it.

Here's the thing. Alan is not even vaguely threatening. His voice is quiet, but not in a lethal-calm way. He sounds uncertain.

And physically? I could take this guy easily. Not that I've gotten in a fight since grade two, but I'm in pretty good shape and I don't sit behind a desk all day.

Alan, on the other hand, *does* look like he has a desk job.

"Dammit," he mutters. "Clearly I have some work to do on the protective-older-brother routine."

"Yeah, you do," I say good-naturedly.

"I never used to interfere in my sisters' lives, but after what happened to Valerie, with her ex and her career..." He shakes his head. "I don't want her to go through that again, okay? Just treat her well, that's all."

"Of course. I would never think of doing otherwise."

He gives me a wary smile. "I hear you're a doctor."

I'm about to protest, then remember my act. "Yep. A pediatrician. That's me." The less said about my supposed career, the better. I don't know jack shit about being a doctor. Perhaps I should do a little research.

"How interesting." Alan taps his fingers on the table. "It's as though Valerie found you in a catalogue."

My gut clenches. "What do you mean by that?"

"Oh, just that you're exactly what our mother would want for her, that's all."

I shrug and try to play it cool. "What do you do?"

"I'm a professor."

"Ah."

Valerie steps out of Ginger Scoops and walks over to us. I can't help but smile when I see her, and I remember how it felt to kiss her against the wall and slip my hand inside her bra...

Not now, Peter.

She smiles back at me, then turns to her brother. "You didn't tell me you were coming."

Alan shrugs. "Just a fifteen-minute walk from work. Figured I could use some ice cream on this beautiful day."

"Mm-hmm."

"Actually, he threatened me," I say cheerfully.

"You *what*?" Valerie glares at her brother.

"He told me I better not fuck around on you. Or else. Normal stuff like that."

"If Peter tries anything," Valerie says to Alan, "don't worry, I'll deal with him myself. I'll string him up by his balls and lock him in a room with a rotten durian."

Alan barks out a laugh.

I chuckle, too. I'm not worried, because I'm going to treat Valerie like a queen, and nobody will be stringing anyone up by the balls.

When she sits down, I shift my chair toward hers and wrap my arm around the back of her chair. Part of our act, you know.

"So, you'll never guess what Instruct-Ed did this time," Alan says to Valerie.

She leans forward. "What happened?"

"What on earth is Instruct-Ed?" I ask.

"It's the course management software I'm forced to use." Alan sighs. "It's horrible. And I've discovered that students are able to change the marks on their labs."

"*They can change their own marks?*" Valerie says.

Alan smiles at her vehemence. "Yeah. They can."

"Isn't that exactly what course software is not supposed to do?" I ask.

"That's correct. Now, to be fair, it appears they can only change their marks to zero—they can't give themselves a hundred percent—and when that happens, they complain to me, of course. Three students have done it so far."

"I want to get my hands on that code so badly." Valerie turns to me. "Can you believe this is the most popular course management software in Canada? It has so many bugs, and the software developers seem to have no understanding of what instructors use it for."

I get the feeling Alan and Valerie have had some variation of this conversation many times before. And I understand why.

I can make Valerie smile. I can turn her on. I can help her relax.

But she has a spark in her eye I haven't seen before, and I suddenly understand she *needs* her career back.

She told me she couldn't. She didn't explain any further, but now I know she desperately wants it. She's excited by the idea of making this software better, and it's just course management software that she's never even used before.

I always knew Valerie was brilliant. I swear I could see it from the very beginning, when she bumped into me with her durian ice cream and released a string of curse words. I was drawn to her; I knew she was intelligent and magnificent.

I just wasn't sure what she was meant to use that brilliance for.

Until now.

Something awful must have happened to push her away from her career, and somehow, I'm going to help her fix it.

But I'm not going to push her to tell me before she wants to.

The next afternoon, I return to Ginger Scoops for some ice cream. Vietnamese coffee and green tea-strawberry, perhaps?

No. Green tea and coffee would clash.

In my opinion, it's best to pick flavors that complement each other at least a little. I came to this conclusion after having mango and amaretto gelato together, a combination I do not recommend.

I step up to the counter and Valerie smiles at me. "What can I get you on this fine October afternoon?" she asks, acting all proper, as though she doesn't know what it's like to have my erection pressing between her legs.

"What would you recommend with Vietnamese coffee?"

"Maybe chocolate-raspberry?"

"Sounds good. I'll have it in a bubble waffle."

She pours the batter into the waffle maker then returns to the cash register. Her hand is resting on the counter, and I idly trace circles over the back of it.

I want to make all your dreams come true.

She's wearing an apron over a simple blue T-shirt, and she's truly stunning. I can't believe I get to touch her.

I want to take you to bed and make you feel so good. When you're ready, of course.

We exchange a private grin.

I love falling in love.

The chimes above the door tinkle, and I step away from Valerie, cursing the new customers for interrupting our moment.

It's a young man and woman, about our age. The man gives Valerie a curious look, and I'm immediately on guard.

"Valerie Chow?" he says. "Is that you?"

She stiffens, just for a second, and I don't think he notices.

"Brendan," she says pleasantly. "Hi."

"You work here?" Perhaps it's my imagination, but there's a slight sneer in his voice.

"I do. What can I get for you today?"

He turns to the woman next to him. "Valerie and I went to U of T together."

"We sure did," Valerie says, with a complete lack of enthusiasm.

"She was one of the smartest kids in the class," he says. "I'm surprised you're not working in the field anymore."

"I'm working at an ice cream shop because that's what I want to do." Her expression is hard. Resolute. "It was my best friend's dream to open this place. What about you?"

I can hear the reluctance dripping from her voice. She's trying to be polite, but this Brendan guy, he's content to ignore her tone. He babbles on about some software company he's working for, like he's a hotshot or something. Even the woman standing next to him—his girlfriend?—looks annoyed.

I'm about to interrupt this idiocy, but then the woman says, "For God's sake, Brendan, nobody wants to hear about your job." She steps toward the counter. "I will have a single scoop of strawberry-lychee sorbet, please."

The two of them get their ice cream and are outside by the time my bubble waffle is ready. Valerie folds it into a cone. "Which flavors did you want again?" Her voice wavers.

"Vietnamese coffee and chocolate-raspberry," I say.

"Right, of course."

"It doesn't matter what that idiot thinks. Even his girlfriend knows he's an asshole. There's nothing wrong with not using your degree. Like me."

"I know. I just…"

"Unlike me, you want to use it."

She nods and hands over my ice cream. Our fingers brush, and I have to restrain myself from touching her further.

"Why don't you ask questions?" she says.

"I ask plenty of questions. May I kiss you?"

She chuckles. "You know what I mean."

"I don't ask questions because you don't seem ready to answer them, not because I don't want to know everything about you."

"Thank you," she says. "And yes, you may kiss me, as soon as I'm able to take a break."

"I look forward to it."

Later, after I've kissed her and returned home, I do a little Googling and find something that will definitely make her smile. Not long ago, I would have been highly disturbed that such a place existed, but now, I'm glad. I can't wait to take her there.

As I said, I love falling in love.

It makes you see the world in a different way.

Chapter 12

Valerie

My phone buzzes and I jump up from the kitchen table, where I've been drinking tea with my mother and helping sort her button collection, which she keeps in a blue cookie tin.

"He's here," I say, unable to stop my heart from beating quickly.

"You will be home for dinner?"

"I don't know, Mom. Probably not, but he didn't tell me where we're going. It's a surprise."

She clucks her tongue. "He should have given you some idea so you know what to wear!" She frowns at my jeans and off-the-shoulder black shirt, which I have paired with a simple silver necklace.

"I'm sure if I needed to dress up, he would have told me."

"You know men. They never think of these things. Your father would wear socks with sandals to the office if I'd let him. Anyway, I will probably be out when you get home. Going to Connie's after dinner."

"Oh, so you think you'll be out later than me on a Monday night?"

"Yes, because Peter is a good boy, and he will bring you home before midnight."

"And you are not a good girl, so you will be out after midnight, gambling and gossiping with your friends?"

My mom laughs. "I worked so hard, all my life. Now it's my time to shine! I can do whatever I like. My only job now is to make sure my children marry good people, but that is not a full-time job, and I think you are doing well, yes? You don't look so down in the dumps these days. He's good for you."

"He's a freaking pediatrician. That's all you care about."

"Aiyah! Why do you say that? It's not true." She pats my hand. "Now go! Don't keep him waiting."

"The reason I'm keeping him waiting is because you're still talking."

"Ah, blame it all on your poor mother."

I give her a look, then wave before I dash to the door and put on a pair of black flats.

Peter is parked in the driveway. When I slide into the passenger's seat of his old Toyota, I can't help touching him. I place my hand on his shoulder and grin.

For so many months, it felt like I couldn't truly enjoy myself or look forward to things. Sure, I hung out with my friends, but it wasn't quite the same.

The last few weeks, however, have been different.

"Where are you taking me?" I ask as I buckle my seatbelt.

He backs out of the driveway. "I'm not telling you. We'll be there in twenty minutes. You can make it that long, can't you?"

"Fine, fine," I mutter, making a show of being annoyed. "If I must."

"You look really good tonight. Too bad I have to keep my eyes on the road."

"Yeah, too bad I don't want to be roadkill."

"You say the most romantic things." He squeezes my thigh, then returns his hand to the steering wheel.

Twenty minutes later, we pull up to a plaza in Richmond Hill. Most of the signs have Chinese in addition to English.

There's a congee restaurant, a small grocery store, and a smartphone repair place.

My heart sinks. It's your average Chinese plaza with your average businesses. Maybe he wants to take me to the congee restaurant—I don't mind, I like congee—but I was expecting something more exciting, since he made a big deal about it being a surprise.

You shouldn't hope too much. That way you won't be disappointed.

Yes, that's a lesson I learned last year. I couldn't deal with the crushing disappointment of having everything ripped away from me, and I didn't dare hope that things would improve.

But I've started to hope again, and that's a dangerous thing.

I think of the envelope in my purse. I wish I hadn't brought it.

"Let's go," Peter says, hopping out of the car. "It's around the other side." He takes my hand and we begin walking. "You okay?"

"Yeah." I swallow. "I'm fine."

We turn the corner. He points to the left, and I follow his gaze, not sure what to expect, but having sufficiently lowered my expectations so that I won't be disappointed.

But when I see the green sign, I burst into laughter.

Why did I ever doubt Peter?

"Doctor Durian," I say, reading the sign.

"That's right. It's a durian dessert shop. It opened last week."

I grab his hand and jog across the parking lot until we reach the shop. It's not very fancy, and there are only a couple of tables in the cramped interior. A faint pungent smell permeates the air, and my mouth starts watering.

It's like heaven.

There's a large menu with pictures. Durian pancakes, durian ice cream, durian buns, durian supreme sundae, durian cake, durian sago, durian smoothie, durian mochi, sticky rice with durian...

"Durian cheesecake!" I point to it and laugh.

Peter's nose is wrinkled slightly—how does he look so damn cute with his nose wrinkled?—but he's smiling.

"Order whatever you like," he says. "My treat."

Peter absolutely hates durian and can't stand the smell, but he's brought me here, and he looks happy.

Because he likes making *me* happy.

"Apparently the durian pancakes are really good," he says. "So I've heard."

"Will you get anything?"

"They have a few non-durian items."

"How shocking!"

He laughs. "Mango pancakes, maybe."

In addition to all the food, there are a few greeting cards with cartoon durians, as well as postcards showing the fruit growing on trees. Another postcard depicts some kind of durian festival in Malaysia.

"Can I help you?" asks the woman behind the counter.

It takes me a solid five minutes to figure out what to get. It all looks so good. A little on the expensive side, though—durian isn't cheap.

Eventually, I decide on the durian pancakes, and Peter orders the mango ones.

We take a seat at one of the rickety tables by the window, and the woman brings our food over a few minutes later. She sets a square white plate with two yellow pancakes, stuffed and folded into rectangles, in front of me. They look exactly like the ones I had in Hong Kong many years ago, an experience I haven't forgotten because they were the most delicious thing I've ever eaten.

I bugged Peter about taking pictures at the Thai rolled ice cream shop, but this time, I'm the one snapping photos. I take several of my food after it arrives, then cut one of the pancakes in half and take some more. Peter insists on getting a photo of me and my food, too.

Then, at long last, I have a bite of pancake filled with whipped cream and durian flesh, and the taste explodes in my mouth.

I don't know how to describe the taste of durian. It's a bit like a cross between creamy banana and mango with a hint of caramel, yet not too sweet? But really, there's nothing else like it.

I put down my fork after my first bite.

"So good," I say to Peter. "Do you want to try some?"

"I've already tried durian ice cream and durian bun in your presence. I think I'll pass."

"True. This would be wasted on you, and it doesn't deserve to be wasted." I lovingly pet my uneaten durian pancake, and he laughs.

"Perhaps I'd like durian if I'd first been exposed to it when I was young," he says. "Oh, well. It's too late now."

"How are your mango pancakes?"

"Very good, but not as orgasmic as yours. I'm glad you're enjoying it."

I slide my chair around the table so that I'm sitting closer to him, and with one hand on his thigh, I savor the rest of my durian pancakes.

"Oh my God, that was delicious," I say, setting down my fork.

"Do you want anything else?"

"I shouldn't, but maybe I'll get a durian smoothie to go."

"Uh-uh. No way are you bringing that into my car."

"Aw, come on!" I punch him lightly on the shoulder.

But I won't press. He hates the smell of durian, and although a durian smoothie wouldn't be as bad as taking a fresh durian into his car, I understand.

"I'll get a small one," I say, "and I'll finish it before we get in your car, don't worry."

Once I have my durian smoothie in hand, we wander around the exterior of the plaza, my other hand in his.

"You know," I say, shaking my plastic cup, "I'm tempted to pour some on you."

"Why on earth would you do that?"

"Because when you got durian ice cream on your shirt, you couldn't whip it off fast enough."

He barks out a laugh that reverberates all through my body.

"Darling," he says, "if you want me to take off my shirt, you just have to ask. You don't need to resort to spilling a durian smoothie on me."

"Hmm." I let go of him and slide my hand under the hem of his shirt so I can feel his warm skin.

We have noodles for dinner at a nearby restaurant, and then I tell Peter to take us to a deserted parking lot, which he does. It's not entirely empty, but there are only a couple of other cars, and it's dark out now.

Good enough for me.

"What do you want to do in a parking lot?" he asks, raising his eyebrows.

"First..." I dig into my purse and produce the envelope I've been carrying around all evening. "For you."

"For me?" His lips curve upward.

When I nod, he opens the envelope and slides out the card.

On the front is a photo of two golden retriever puppies cuddling. I went to Moonbeam Messages yesterday to look for the perfect card to give Peter, but now, I feel uncertain. I only gave Stephen cards for Valentine's Day and our anniversary. Never a "just because" card with puppies.

Peter opens it.

You make me feel comfy is the printed message inside. I haven't written anything else, aside from the salutation and signature.

But it's a goddamn puppy card. This isn't the kind of thing I do.

I'm about to grab it back, but then Peter says, "I love it."

A part of me still wants to say, *It doesn't mean anything. It's just part of our act.* But I don't. Because that's not true.

Instead, I let the words hang between us.

"Let's go to the backseat," he says. "I think I know what you want to do in a parking lot. I feel like I'm in high school again."

"Yeah? I never did anything like this when I was in high school."

"There's a first time for everything."

"You'll be happy to know that I had a breath mint, so I shouldn't smell like durian."

"I would kiss you even if you'd just eaten a whole durian."

"That's the most romantic thing anyone's ever said to me." I put a hand to my chest, then hop out of the car and climb into the backseat.

Peter pulls me into his lap so I'm straddling him. I press myself against his chest and wind my arms around him. He feels so good against me. So right.

"How about this," he murmurs. "I'll pretend I just got durian ice cream on my shirt. Sound like a plan?"

Without waiting for an answer, he pulls his shirt over his head. I can't see him as well as I'd like in the dim light, but I still gasp.

"Good gasp or bad gasp?" he chuckles, his mouth close to my ear, his voice confident.

"Good gasp," I say.

I run my hands over his abs, up to his shoulders, then down his arms. I'm in the backseat of a car with a very fine specimen of man, that's for sure, and he radiates a sizzling heat. Just touching him like this is enough to quicken my breath.

I remove my own shirt, then my bra.

"Valerie." He takes my breast in his hand, stroking my nipple to a tight peak.

And then he takes it in his mouth, and I gasp once more. He licks a circle around the tip, and yes, that's so good.

When he lifts his head from my breast, I press my chest against his, my bare skin against his. It feels divine.

"Fuck," I say. "Fuck."

"I like when you swear. You know, I read an article the other day that said swearing is linked to intelligence." He pauses, and when he speaks again, his voice is soft. "What do you want to do tonight? As much or as little as you wish, it's all good."

I rub myself against his erection, and he growls low in his throat.

"I have to tell you something first." I swallow. I don't *have* to tell him this, but I want him to know how sexy I find him. "The night we made out in Graffiti Alley? I tried to get myself off when I got home."

"Tried but didn't succeed?"

"My mom interrupted me," I say morosely. "And in my shock, I threw the vibrator across the room. Luckily, it didn't break anything."

He chuckles, but his gaze is intense on mine. He places his fingers at the top of my jeans. "I can take care of that for you tonight."

"Peter, I…"

God, I feel messed up. He's wonderful, and I want him, and yet the idea of him sliding his fingers inside me… No. Not yet. I'm comfortable with him, enough to admit that I masturbated, but not quite *that* comfortable.

"We don't have to," he says.

"I'd rather do you instead. Is that okay?"

"It is."

"It's easier for me to give than receive. For now. I need to be in control."

I unbutton his jeans, reach into his boxers, and grasp his cock—and that's enough to make me shudder. He's so hard, but his skin is soft and velvety, and God, I can feel how much he wants me. He's already fisting his hands at his sides. When I move my hand up and down a few times, his jaw tightens.

I kiss his mouth, exploring with my lips and tongue, and squirm in his lap, wanting to feel him between my legs. It would be so easy to take off my jeans and panties and tell him to do whatever he wants to me, but I'm not ready for that, not yet.

I continue to kiss him as I stroke him, reveling in every little sound he makes. I try to tell him, with my body, everything I cannot say.

I didn't think I could trust a man again, but I'm starting to trust you.

With you, I'm learning to have fun again.

I slide off his lap and kneel on the seat beside him. "I'm going to suck you off," I say matter-of-factly. "Is that okay?"

He grabs a handful of my hair and nods.

There's a bead of pre-cum at the tip; I lick it then take as much of him in my mouth as I can. He tastes slightly salty, and I relish the taste. It's good to do this simply because I want to.

This is for *me*.

And him, of course. Because I want to bring him pleasure. So much pleasure. I hadn't let myself want or hope, but then I barreled into him at Ginger Scoops.

My hand is wrapped around the base of his dick. I move it up as I move my mouth down.

"Valerie."

There's a bite of pain as he tightens his grip on my hair, but I like it, and I like that it will go away at the snap of my fingers if that's what I want.

And he's so hard for me.

"Valerie," he says, "I'm going to…"

I'm suddenly unsure about swallowing, so I release his cock with a *pop* and work him quickly with my hand. It's not long before he comes and my palm is wet and sticky.

He passes me some tissues, and I clean us up and tuck him back into his pants, feeling rather proud of myself.

"What do you want?" he asks, sounding a bit dazed.

"Just hold me." I climb back onto his lap.

We kiss in the backseat of his car, until we hear another car pull into the parking lot. Then he drives me home.

And this time, my mother is still out playing mahjong, and she doesn't interrupt me when I pull out my green vibrator and use it furtively under the covers.

Chapter 13

Peter

It's the holiday Monday. Canadian Thanksgiving.

I'm driving to Valerie's parents' house in Scarborough, with a pear ginger crumble pie and a pumpkin pie from Happy as Pie on the passenger's seat.

Now, I'm usually a pretty easygoing guy who doesn't get too stressed, but right now, I'm freaking the fuck out. Sure, I've already met Valerie's mother and brother, but this is the real test. The family Thanksgiving.

The inconvenient thing about this car? I keep remembering what happened last week. Valerie's mouth on my cock, her hair forming a dark curtain over her face, her hand cupping my balls, her bare breasts bouncing...

Apparently, you take a girl out for durian pancakes and she gives you a blowjob in the backseat of your car. Funny I never figured that out before. I should remember for next time.

Not, of course, that I'm able to think of any other woman while Valerie is gradually letting me further and further into her life.

I'm desperate to slide my fingers into her wetness, to lick her until she cries out and comes against my mouth. To feel her pussy gripping my cock.

Maybe this week...

Stop. Focus. Get in character.

Yeah, I need my brain in full working order to play my part. Not that it requires all that much acting. Because I *am* crazy about Valerie, and being a little affectionate with her is second nature.

I just have to remember not to be *too* affectionate.

And I have to remember that I'm a doctor and they will ask me about doctor-ly things. Supposedly, I'm now two years into my four-year residency—I looked up how long residency is for pediatrics here—and will be finished the summer after next.

I also have to remember not to make any comments about my actual job, or reveal the details of my mother's art—which is something I'm used to hiding from my girlfriends' parents.

But pretending I'm a doctor...that's a new one.

My parents would laugh their asses off.

I saw my family yesterday. They'd originally wanted to do Thanksgiving dinner on Monday, but I told them I was going to a family dinner with the woman I'm seeing. My sister, Mackenzie, laughed and started singing Britney Spears's "Oops!...I Did It Again." She likes to make fun of me for all the girlfriends I've had.

Thirteen girlfriends in twelve years isn't *that* many, is it?

Anyway, I told my family about Valerie, but not about the fake relationship part and the fact that her family thinks I'm a pediatrician.

I park on the street by her parents' house, and before I climb out of the car, I pull out the card she gave me from the glove compartment.

I looked at it during every lunch break last week. It always makes me smile.

Alright, self. You are an intelligent doctor with an excellent bedside manner, and Valerie's family will love you.

With the pies in one hand, I ring the doorbell.

A minute later, Valerie opens the door, looking breathless and beautiful. It's a warm October day, and she's wearing jeans and a short-sleeve blouse.

"Hey," she says.

I haven't seen her since Friday—we spent a couple of hours together after she finished work—and I've missed her, even though it's only been three days.

I bend down and plant a chaste kiss on her cheek.

"Hey," I whisper, then straighten.

"Peter!" Cynthia bursts into the front hall. "So good to see you again. You brought dessert, yes? Valerie said you were bringing two pies. You bake, as well as being a doctor?" She beams at me.

"Mom!" Valerie says. "We went through this many times. I asked him to bring dessert from Sarah's shop, Happy as Pie. He didn't make them himself. He doesn't bake."

"Actually, I do."

"You bake?" Valerie asks, as though this is truly unbelievable information.

"A little. Cookies, muffins, a bunch of things."

All of this is true. I'm only lying about my career.

"When do you have the time?" Cynthia turns to Valerie. "He is perfect."

I smile, but inside, I feel a twitch of unease.

What would Cynthia think if she knew I'm not a doctor? Would she still be happy with me dating her daughter?

A young woman, who bears a slight resemblance to Valerie, bounds into the hallway. She stops suddenly, her mouth open in a small circle.

"Wow," she whispers, and she seems to be struggling to find her voice. "You're even better looking than in the picture."

"I can't believe it," Valerie says. "You practically rendered my sister speechless. Her name is Sabrina, by the way."

Sabrina glares at Valerie, who circles her arm possessively around my waist.

I don't mind. Not at all.

I put my arm around her, too.

"Alan isn't here yet," Valerie says. "Dad went out to buy potatoes, because someone"—she looks at Cynthia—"forgot to buy them. Hopefully he can find a store that's open."

"How was I supposed to remember? There were so many things to buy."

"You know, Mom," Valerie says, "a list would be helpful. I don't know why you go grocery shopping without a list."

"What would be the fun in that?"

"Grocery shopping isn't fun."

"That's what you think." Cynthia takes my arm. "Come in and make yourself comfortable."

Well, here we go.

An hour and a half later, we're sitting around the dining room table, which is loaded with roast turkey, dressing, gravy, mashed potatoes, squash, cranberries, and bok choy. I have a sip of my tea before I cut into my turkey.

"So, Sabrina," I say, "you're at U of T, right? What are you studying?"

"English and film studies," she replies.

I open my mouth to say that I studied English, too, then remember I'm supposed to have a degree in life sciences.

"What do you hope to do after you graduate?" I ask instead.

"Law school. I did really well on the LSAT."

"I guess a lawyer is okay," Cynthia says. "But English! Such a useless thing to study."

"It teaches communication and critical thinking, doesn't it?" I say. "Those are useful."

"You see?" Sabrina turns to her mother, then back to me.

Cynthia sniffs. "I suppose it could be worse. Do you have any siblings, Peter?"

"A younger sister. She's an engineer."

"A doctor and an engineer. Your parents must be proud."

I nod. "They are."

I don't mention that my parents would be proud of me no matter what. Or that they recently went to a nudist beach. Or that the last painting my mom sold was of a vagina with teeth.

"Too bad you don't have any brothers," Sabrina says.

Valerie looks at her sister and shakes her head. She shifts her leg so it's pressed against mine, and I can feel her heat through my khakis.

It's hard to be appropriate in front of her family.

Just think about your parents going to a nudist beach. That will kill your desire.

Yep, it's as effective as usual.

"What year did you graduate from med school?" Alan asks.

"2017," I say.

He turns to his mother. "That's when Daphne's niece finished, isn't it? What's her name—Justine? You know her, Peter?"

"I don't."

How big are med school classes? Maybe two hundred? So it wouldn't be unreasonable for me not to know everyone in my class.

I have a sip of tea, then a bite of turkey with cranberry sauce. "This is delicious."

"Thank you." Cynthia smiles at me

"I helped, too," Sabrina says.

Valerie rolls her eyes. "Oh, come on. All you did was peel the potatoes."

"And make the gravy."

"You stirred it for five seconds. It doesn't count."

"Yes, it does!"

I chuckle. It reminds me of my own family. Mackenzie and I don't bicker as much anymore, but we still tease each other.

The one person who's hardly said a word during this family dinner is Valerie's father. He seems content to eat his food in silence.

"How did you two meet?" Alan asks. "I don't think I've heard the story."

"At the ice cream shop!" Cynthia says. "You have not been paying attention."

"But how, exactly?"

"He was a customer, obviously, and was blown away by her charm and good looks."

Sabrina suppresses a snicker.

I turn to Alan. "I was heading into Ginger Scoops, and Valerie was exiting the patio with a double scoop of ice cream. Neither of us was paying attention. She ran into me and got durian ice cream all over me."

"So romantic!" Cynthia says.

"And then he whipped off his shirt," Valerie says, "since he was offended by the smell of durian." Her eyes go wide and she covers her mouth. "Shit. I didn't mean to say...you know..."

I rather enjoy Valerie's stammering, though I'm a touch embarrassed that she mentioned the whipping-off-my-shirt part. "I hate durian, you see."

"Ah, so you have a flaw after all!" Cynthia says.

"No, durian is nasty." Sabrina looks at me with adoring eyes. "You. Took off. Your shirt?"

"Um," I say.

"Sabrina, will you go fill up the gravy boat?" Cynthia asks.

Sabrina rolls her eyes but does as requested.

Under the table, Valerie squeezes my leg, and I can't help smiling at her touch.

The rest of dinner goes okay, and the pies from Happy as Pie are better than anything I could have made, that's for sure. Sabrina cuts me an extra-big piece of pumpkin pie.

After dessert, I offer to do dishes.

"No, you're a guest," Valerie says. "I will help my mom."

"I can help," Alan says. "You can hang out with Peter."

Cynthia shakes her head. "Let Peter do it. He offered."

Soon, it's just Cynthia and me in the kitchen, and it appears she wants the two of us to do dishes together so she can have a private conversation with me.

"You are being so proper with Valerie," she says.

I manage to keep a straight face, despite thinking of the blowjob I got in my car.

"Proper," I say. "Yes."

"Every time, you bring her back here for the night."

I didn't bring her home until two in the morning one time, but we've never spent the whole night together, it's true.

"Valerie is an adult," Cynthia says. "Yes, she lives at home, but if she stays over at your place, that is fine. I won't say anything."

Is she giving me permission to sleep with her daughter?

"I'm not stupid," Cynthia continues. "I know you are probably doing it. She is a grown-up, and she already lived with a man for three years. You know that, right?"

I didn't know how long it had lasted, but yes, I knew.

I nod and focus on drying the plate in my hands.

"I hope she keeps you around. You are a nice boy. I'm glad you were able to spend Thanksgiving with us. I know you must work hard, being at the hospital all the time."

I'm pleased with myself for having pulled off this fake/not-so-fake boyfriend thing well enough. I haven't accidentally talked about my job in landscaping, and Cynthia still likes me.

But if I'm going to be Valerie's boyfriend for real...well, I can't hide the truth of my job forever, can I?

And I suspect that conversation will not go well.

Chapter 14

Valerie

I'm going home with Peter. I've decided.

I don't care what my family thinks. I'm twenty-six years old, and as far as they know, he's my boyfriend.

We're sitting side-by-side on the couch now, my arm around his shoulders. It's torture not to be able to do more with him. Ever since last Monday, it's been torture, in fact. I use my goddamn vibrator every night and think of him.

A week ago, I couldn't imagine letting him do everything to me, but that's changed.

I'm ready.

I also have the urge to scandalize my family, and to send a message to my sister that yes, this man is mine. It's annoying to watch her batting her eyelashes at Peter. She never even liked Asian guys before, and now she's smitten by my boyfriend?

Uh-uh. She doesn't get to have him.

I tell Peter that I'll be back in a few minutes, then go upstairs to pack a small overnight bag. Just as I'm zipping it up, my mother knocks on the door and enters.

"Ah, you're going to spend the night with him. Good."

"Good?"

"Yes, you must keep him happy, or he will go elsewhere."

Oh God. Not this again.

Fortunately, she doesn't call me a very expensive, delicious piece of meat this time.

At ten o'clock, Mom gives Peter a large bag of leftovers, and the two of us head out. Every time we come to a stoplight, he puts his hand on my leg.

"Thank you for coming tonight," I say.

"It was no trouble," he murmurs. "None at all."

"My mother loves you and no longer thinks I'm a complete failure of a daughter."

He glances at me. "Regardless of me, you are not a failure."

"She encouraged me to spend the night with you."

"Yeah, she told me when we were washing dishes that it would be fine."

I make a face. "Damn, this is awkward."

Once we're alone in his apartment, though, my family disappears from my mind, and there is only Peter. Peter, who has always been so lovely to me and went along with my scheme to pretend he was a doctor in front of my family.

He slides his arms around my waist. "Tell me what you want tonight."

"Everything." I swallow. "I want everything."

He grins. "But feel free to stop me at any time, okay? We don't need to have sex just because your mother is encouraging it."

I roll my eyes. "Can we forget about my mother now?"

He picks me up, and I squeak in surprise. He carries me to the bedroom and sets me down on the bed, and then he climbs on top of me and kisses me.

This is the first time we've kissed while lying down, and it feels pretty damn spectacular, his weight pressing me into the mattress. But I need to touch his skin, so I pull off his T-shirt. He's built and solid, but not freaky-chiseled, and I think he's perfect.

If I hadn't made up a fake boyfriend named Peter—thank you, *To All the Boys I've Loved Before*—the day before we ran into each other, would we have started anything?

I doubt it.

The world works in interesting ways.

Okay, now I'm getting philosophical when I'm supposed to be getting freaky.

The problem is, as much as I love touching him, as much as I love his lips on me, I really struggle to quiet my mind when I'm in bed with a man.

Even Peter.

He pulls me up, just long enough to remove my shirt and bra, and now we're half-clothed together.

"You're beautiful," he breathes, his gaze raking over my brownish nipples and smallish breasts and acne scars.

Stop thinking about those things, Valerie. You're beautiful. He said it, so it must be true.

He presses a kiss to my neck, then one to my collarbone, then one to the slope of my breast...and finally one to my nipple.

I gasp.

Everything he does is wonderful. He has a way with my body. Or maybe he's just really good with women in general, having had all those girlfriends?

Stop thinking about other women, Valerie!

To distract myself, I reach for the zipper on his pants. I pull them off and toss them on the floor, and now he's only wearing his boxers.

He lies on his side next to me, a crooked smile on his face, and trails his fingers over my breasts.

My breath comes faster.

I'm in bed with a guy. The first guy I've been with since all that bad shit happened. I want Peter, but I'm still freaking out, and oh my God, why am I so bad at intimacy?

Well, I'll just have to get through it. I tug off my jeans and underwear and throw them on the floor. I'm entirely naked now.

"Mm." He climbs on top of me again and rubs himself against me as he kisses his way down my neck. "You good?"

"Yes. I'm good."

He runs his hands all over me, my breasts, my ass, my hips, my stomach. His touch is firm, but somehow reverent. He's so fucking sweet, and he...

He slips his hand between my legs.

He's probably expecting me to be wet for him. But...

"Why don't I give you another blowjob?" I say, removing his hand from my body. I glance at the tent his cock is making in his boxers and reach toward him, but he stills me.

"If you're not interested, you don't have to do anything today. We can just sleep beside each other, or I can sleep on the couch, if you prefer."

"Can't let you have blue balls."

"Yes, you can. It's not a problem, or I can take care of myself. Don't worry about me."

When we made out in the alley and in the backseat of the car, I wasn't such a basket case. Perhaps because I knew we weren't going to go any further, I could just let go. But now, it's different.

"I want to have sex, but I'm very bad at it," I blurt out.

"I find that hard to believe."

"It's difficult for me to just let go and be intimate with someone. Also, I'm not good at getting off. Or getting wet, as you may have noticed. There's nothing wrong with me—I've been to the doctor—and it's not like I don't get wet at all, just not as much as other women, from what I understand. So, like, you might think it's because I'm not in the mood or I'm not sufficiently attracted to you, but I am. My body just doesn't cooperate, and it'll probably make you frustrated. And it's extra bad now because I'm stressing out about it."

"Well, there's a very easy solution." He reaches into his bedside table and pulls out a bottle of lube. "Now, is there a way for me to get you off?"

"Only using a vibrator. Please don't take it as a personal challenge and spend half an hour going down on me, convinced you're different. Don't hold off during sex, waiting for me to come." I reach into my bag and pull out my lime-green vibrator and slap it on the night table, my cheeks heating in mortification.

I can't help thinking about what happened with Stephen. He told me he had to go elsewhere because I was too difficult in bed. He said I wasn't meeting his needs, couldn't meet his needs. I know he's a piece of shit, but he gets in my head sometimes.

I've always been a bit neurotic when it comes to sex, and now it's worse.

This is the first time I've tried to have such a conversation before sex. I figure it's better than Peter fucking me until it hurts, determined to get me off, and me faking an orgasm in desperation.

But I've ruined the mood. It's my first time with a new guy, and we should be overcome with waves of passion, not having an awkward talk.

Peter doesn't deserve this.

Yet it turns out that, once again, Peter is unflappable.

"It's okay," he whispers, "I can work with that, though you might have to give me some guidance, okay? Don't be afraid to tell me what feels good and what doesn't."

"You could find someone who's less of a weirdo and isn't lying to her parents about your profession."

"I could, but I want you."

It's hard to believe, even though I can see that in his eyes, feel it in the way he's caressing my body.

"You still want to do this tonight?" he asks.

"Yes."

"It might take a few times to get it right, but I'm happy to practice." He winks at me. "Don't worry about a thing. It's all okay, I promise."

For a long time, we just kiss. Eventually, he reaches for the lube, squirts a tiny bit on his fingers, and rubs his thumb over my clit. I arch toward him.

He runs a finger over my slit before slipping it inside me. "How's that?"

"It's good."

"Now show me how you like it." He hands me my vibrator.

My cheeks flame. "I'm not sure I can do this in front of you."

"Alright. Some other time." He turns the vibrator on and starts to use it on my clit, his finger still inside me. His cock peeks out from his boxers, and I reach for it. He's rock-hard, which is a surprise, given how weird I've been.

Relax, Valerie. Just relax.

And slowly, as he keeps touching me and pressing kisses all over my body, I'm able to relax. When I pump his cock a few times, he pulls my hand away.

"You have to stop, or I won't last."

He's this turned on. For me.

Don't act so surprised, Valerie. You're hot shit.

I can't help snickering at my thoughts. They're all over the place.

"What is it?" he murmurs.

I shake my head.

He smiles at me, then asks, "Can I go down on you? Do you like that?"

"Yeah. I just can't quite get all the way there from oral sex."

"Okay." He turns off the vibrator and slides down my body until his mouth is at my crotch. He licks along my entrance before sucking on my clit. He slips a second finger inside me, providing just the right amount of fullness...for now.

I sink into the mattress. My swirling mess of thoughts is starting to calm.

I want it to be perfect with him, but our first time together is unlikely to be perfect.

And that's okay.

It's him and it's me, and we can figure it out.

He adds a third finger. I'm not used to having so much inside my body, not used to the touch of anyone but me and my plastic friend, but he's preparing me to take his cock, and God, that thought is hot.

I thrust my hands through his hair and hold his head against me as he continues to lick me. It feels good now, really good, and I squirm against him.

He slides up my body, keeping his fingers in me, and kisses my lips. I taste myself, and somehow, that's particularly intimate.

Peter strokes in and out of me as we kiss, and every press of his lips against mine seems just a little different. Some seem to say, *you are wonderful just the way you are*; others say, *I want to be inside you so badly*.

I have never enjoyed kissing a man so much.

"May I fuck you now?" he asks.

"Yes," I say.

He reaches into his bedside table again and produces a foil packet.

My heart thumps in my chest with anticipation. There's still a twinge of nervousness—I'm not surprised he couldn't get rid of that entirely—but I know this is going to be okay.

He rolls on the condom. It's lubricated, but he squeezes some more lube on his hand and rubs it on his cock before guiding the tip to my entrance.

"Do you want it like this?" he asks. "Or another position?"

"This is good."

He pushes in slowly, watching my face the whole time. I feel like he can see everything about me, yet that doesn't make him turn away. He keeps going until he's fully seated within me.

It's an odd sensation after not having a man inside me for so long. Not unpleasant, but not entirely pleasurable...yet.

But I trust it will feel good soon.

I wrap my legs around his hips and press my body up to his, wanting to feel all that I can of him, this man who doesn't just put up with me, but likes me for who I am.

He thrusts shallowly a few times and slowly increases his speed.

For so long, I couldn't bear the thought of doing this with another man, yet here I am. I kiss him everywhere I can, no pattern to my touches—I can't think clearly enough for that.

"God, Valerie...God."

And I revel in the fact that I can make him unravel.

We move in harmony for a while, and then I roll us over so I'm on top. I sit up straight, playing with my breasts, fondling my nipples, watching him watch me.

"Yes," he breathes. "Yes."

I enjoy this simply for what it is. I don't think about reaching a peak that I've never reached from this act; I just enjoy the moment.

He slams his hips up to meet mine, and I gasp.

"Do that again," I say.

He pumps into me a few more times. "I'm going to…" A few frantic thrusts, and then he's crying out my name.

I fall on top of him, my chest against his, as he comes, his entire body shaking beneath mine. I'm in awe of myself, in awe that I could do this to him.

But he's not done.

When I lie on my back beside him, he idly slides his fingers between my folds. Eventually, he picks up the vibrator, turns it on, and touches it to my clit.

I'm so sensitive that I nearly come right away, but not quite.

"Let me show you," I murmur, taking the toy from him. I increase the speed slightly and use it on myself, not as self-conscious as I was before.

"Got it." He kisses my mouth and plays with my breast as he uses the vibrator on me, just how I like it, and I grip the sheet in my hands.

Oh my God. *Oh my God.*

Sensation overwhelms me, flooding every part of my body, and I scream.

Oh, how I scream.

Chapter 15

Peter

I SING AS I stir the wet and dry ingredients together.

Then I remember that Valerie is still sleeping, so I stop. I don't want to disturb her.

I'll wake her up before I head to work, but that's not for nearly an hour. I got up earlier than usual because I have some things to prepare for her.

This will be her first Tuesday in forever without work. Chloe shortened the hours of Ginger Scoops after Thanksgiving, and it's now closed Monday through Wednesday, so Valerie has nothing to do today.

Nothing except the plans I have for her.

I grin when I think of how thrilled she'll be. I sure hope she'll be thrilled, anyway.

The batter now mixed just enough to combine, I pour it into the muffin pan and pop it in the preheated oven. The key to fluffy muffins? Don't overmix the batter.

I wasn't lying when I said I could bake.

By seven thirty, everything is ready, and I return to the bedroom to get dressed and wake Valerie. She's curled up on her side, near the edge of the bed.

She was affectionate—very affectionate—after we had sex. We lay in bed, just cuddling and kissing, for an hour, but when it was time for sleep, she rolled far away from me.

Which, to be honest, was a bit of a relief. I love snuggling, don't get me wrong, but I have a hard time falling asleep when in physical contact with someone, so I'm glad we agree on this point.

I smile as I look at her. She definitely has some sex hair going on.

In fact, I haven't been able to stop smiling since we did it.

She said she was bad at sex, but as expected, that was complete garbage. I bet her asshole live-in boyfriend is to blame for most of her insecurities.

Sure, she doesn't orgasm easily, but that doesn't mean she's bad at sex. I'll just have to do a careful job of learning how she responds and what she likes, but I'm totally up for that.

And God, she can have one hell of an orgasm. I was almost ready to go again after I saw her body arch in the throes of exquisite pleasure.

None of my exes ever orgasmed quite like *that*.

Not that I've spent much time thinking about those women, because Valerie is all I want now. I've met her family and I've had her in my bed. And sure, there's that pesky issue of her parents thinking I'm a pediatrician, but otherwise, everything is going swimmingly.

I press a kiss to her temple. "Valerie, wake up."

Chapter 16

Valerie

I CRACK OPEN AN eye. An unfamiliar alarm clock tells me it's seven thirty in the morning. Ginger Scoops never opens before noon, so I'm rarely awake at this time. Why…?

"Valerie." Someone's shaking me.

Peter.

Right. I slept with my fake boyfriend last night.

Although I can't say it feels "fake" anymore.

He probably wants me to get up so he can go to work, though I hate the idea of heading back to my parents' house in morning rush hour, then hanging out with my mother all day.

"I have plans for you," he says. When I try to pull him into bed with me, he laughs. He lifts me up and sets me on my feet. "Let me show you."

He leads me into the kitchen, and I can't deny it smells amazing in here. Was he baking before I got up?

Nah, that would be ridiculous.

But then I see the rack of muffins.

"Fresh pineapple-carrot muffins," he says, then taps a plastic container. "This is homemade granola. You can have it with the yogurt or soy milk in the fridge. There's also orange juice, strawberries, and blueberries. Here's the French press, all set up for you with the coffee grounds. You like coffee, right? If you want tea, here's the cupboard with the tea and teapot. If you want wine..."

"Wine? I don't need wine for breakfast, Peter."

"Ah, but I didn't plan on you staying just for breakfast. I thought you could stay all day."

"But you'll be at work."

"Yep. You'll have the whole apartment to yourself." He spreads his arms wide. "All for you. You can use my TV to watch Netflix, or read any of my books." He gestures to his bookshelves. Since he was an English major, it's not surprising that he has a lot of books. "Or have a bubble bath. I got some supplies. They're under the sink in the bathroom."

This is all very thoughtful, but I'm a bit confused, and it must show on my face.

"You said you were tired of being around people all the time," he explains. "You wish you could live alone. This is the best I could do. You can introvert it up for the day, and I'll be back at five."

Oh.

"This is too much," I whisper.

"Nonsense. I'm just letting you enjoy my empty apartment for a while. You can use my laptop, too. I wrote the password down on a notepad." He pauses. "Do you not like it?"

Peter usually has a calm confidence about him, but now, some uncertainty has crept into his voice.

"It's wonderful," I tell him.

In fact, it's the nicest thing anyone has ever done for me.

He gives me a hesitant smile. "My extra keys are on the kitchen table. Just text me if you need anything. I might not reply right away, but I'll check my phone regularly. I can talk to your mother, if you like, and tell her you won't be home this morning."

"No, that's not necessary. I'll text her myself."

And then I'll have a full day—nine hours or so—with no one to make demands of me. With no obligations to be social. It's overwhelming.

In a good way. Like that orgasm last night.

My cheeks heat at the memory.

Peter grins. "You're free to masturbate in my bathtub, if you like. Just be sure to tell me about it afterward."

"Peter! I wouldn't..."

Or maybe I would.

"Dammit," he says softly. "I wish I could watch, but sadly, I have to go to work, like, five minutes ago, and this day is for *you*."

"But you didn't know I was staying over until last night."

"I had hopes, though."

I stand on my toes and kiss him goodbye, and he heads out the door with an easy gait.

I feel like he's walked off with my heart.

I'm not super hungry after Thanksgiving dinner last night, but those muffins smell amazing, and if I have a muffin, the granola will feel left out, so I better have some of that, too. I make a small bowl with granola, yogurt, and blueberries, then sit down at the kitchen table with my breakfast and a cup of coffee.

I'm suddenly overcome with a strange urge: to take a picture of my food.

I snap a photo with my phone and send it to Chloe.

> ME: Breakfast at Peter's. He made me muffins.

CHLOE: Aw, that's so romantic! So you finally spent the night together?

ME: Yeah

CHLOE: Good for you. Are you going back to bed again after you finish breakfast?

ME: Nah, he's at work. I'm all alone here for the day.

CHLOE: Oh my God! That's so exciting for you!

I chuckle. Chloe understands how much I've wanted a day alone, even if it's not her idea of fun.

I put down my phone and eat my breakfast. The muffin is warm, and I slather it with butter—no mother to tell me not to. The yogurt and granola are delicious, too, as is the coffee.

It's probably especially delicious since *he* set it up for me. *He* woke up early to bake me muffins!

The thought makes me almost giddy.

After I finish eating and wash my dishes, I look around the room. It's eight o'clock and Peter said he'd be back at five.

Hmm, what should I do?

By two o'clock, I've watched six episodes of a TV show, read for an hour, and eaten leftovers for lunch. I heated up the turkey and a little dressing in a frying pan with lots of gravy. I also helped myself to another muffin—they really are delicious.

Now, I'm sitting at the kitchen table, another cup of coffee in front of me, enjoying the light in Peter's apartment at this time of day.

All of a sudden, a strange urge comes over me.

I picture myself sitting here with my laptop, working on some code. The joy of *finally* figuring out a problem and fixing a bug.

I like making things, but not building something physical like a chair or table, or sewing a dress. We spend so much time on our computers and phones, and that's what I like to make: software. Something that does what I want it to do.

I haven't had this urge in a long time.

I miss my job.

Of course, my job wasn't exactly what I thought it was—or rather, the people at my job weren't who I thought they were, and afterward, nobody would hire me.

Sure, people talk about getting more women to study STEM, but what we need more than anything is for men to stop chasing out the women who are already there and want to stay. Like me.

Something clenches painfully in my chest.

I take a deep breath and blow on my coffee.

It's okay, it really is. I'm working with my best friend, and I'm fake dating—real dating, perhaps?—an amazing guy who is letting me spend the whole day in his apartment. He baked me muffins and gave me a great orgasm last night, and he didn't even blink at the strange way my body acts.

Something catches my eye on the fridge. I walk over, and sure enough, it's the puppy card I gave Peter, held to the fridge with a caterpillar magnet.

I smile. Life is perfect.

Almost.

Chapter 17

Peter

"Valerie?" I walk into my apartment and hang my keys on the rack by the door.

"In here!" she calls.

Sounds like she's in the washroom, and my heart beats quicker. I suspect she's naked, and Valerie in the nude is the stuff of my dreams.

And yesterday, my reality.

I slip off my shoes and find her partially reclined in the bathtub with a glass of white wine, the smile on her face unlike any I've seen before.

She looks serene.

"Have a good day?" I ask, sitting on the edge of the tub.

"The best."

"What did you do?"

"I didn't communicate with anyone—other than a few texts—and it was glorious."

I'm more social than she is, and I don't understand the intense craving to be alone, but I love giving her what she wants.

"What about you?" she asks. "Trim any hedge labyrinths for rich dudes?"

"Actually, yes." I smile at her. I would love to come home to her every day. Valerie Chow in my bathtub? Yeah, I could certainly get used to that.

She sits up, and water droplets run down the slopes of her breasts.

God, seeing her in the bath is giving me ideas.

"I have to admit something," she says. "I've been in the tub a very long time. I wanted you to come home and find me in the bath, and you took a little longer than I expected."

I chuckle at the same time as my body pumps blood to my cock. "You wanted me to find you in the bath? Why, may I ask, is that?"

"You know why."

"No, I don't. Enlighten me, please."

She shoots me a glare.

I've become quite fond of her glares.

I pull my shirt over my head and toss it on the floor, and I grin at the way her gaze slides over my chest. "You know," I say, "I've been working outside all day. I'm covered in sweat and dirt. I'd better get in there with you so I can get clean."

She laughs as I lower myself into the tub and begin trailing kisses up her neck.

Just before I reach her mouth, she whispers, "This isn't pretend anymore. Not for me."

I take Valerie home after dinner, disappointed I don't get to spend more time with her, but I'll see her again soon. And she's agreed that we are now in a real relationship, which is what I wanted all along.

Yes, things are going well.

Back at my apartment, I pour myself a glass of juice, then notice there's something different about the fridge. Next to the puppy card is a card of two penguins holding hands—or flippers, rather. It's adorable.

I was right about Valerie. Like a durian, she is utter mush inside. Sure, she's complicated and a little spiky and not everyone understands her, but I think I do.

I'm about to open the card when my phone rings.

It's my father.

"Peter," he says, "how was Thanksgiving dinner with your girlfriend's family?"

I can't help smiling when he says "girlfriend."

"It went well," I say.

"I just want to remind you that we leave for Spain on Thursday."

Oh, shit. I forgot about that.

"So you'll stay here and look after Biscuit, right?" Dad asks.

Biscuit is my parents' Bichon Frise. They got her a couple of years ago. My mother had long dreamed of getting a little dog and naming her Biscuit; my father hates the name and voted to call the dog Fred, but eventually, he caved. Sometimes he still calls her Fred to annoy my mom, though.

"Yes," I say. "No problem."

"You don't sound terribly enthusiastic."

"No, no. It's fine."

It just means I'll be heading to my parents' house in Thornhill after work each night, rather than having a shower at my apartment and going to see Valerie at Ginger Scoops.

But we'll manage.

"There's something I have to tell you," Dad says, suddenly serious.

My heart rate kicks up a notch.

"Biscuit is an Instagram star."

Wait. *What?*

"Biscuit is an Instagram star?" I repeat.

"Yes. It was all your mother's idea…" Dad trails off, and a moment later, my mom gets on the phone.

"Hey, Peter," she says. "That's right, Biscuit is quite popular! You see, I found all these Instagram accounts for Bichon Frises, and I thought, 'Well, they're cute, but not as cute as Biscuit,' so I started my own for her." Mom goes on to tell me the Instagram handle, as well as the password. "She has lots of followers, and her fans will be upset if they don't see any pictures of her for ten days. So I was wondering if you'd be able to add a couple of pictures to her account while we're away. Maybe a video?"

"Um. You want me to maintain your dog's Instagram account?"

"Yup, just while we're gone. You'll be looking after Biscuit anyway, and she's bound to do sweet things."

Well. My parents have Facebook accounts, but I never expected them to be on Instagram. I certainly never expected them to have an account for their pet.

The world is a strange, strange place.

"Uh, yeah, sure. I can do that."

"Thank you! Oh, and just to let you know, there's a new painting in the guest room."

I pinch the bridge of my nose. "Was that really necessary?"

When my sister and I moved out for good, Mom and Dad changed my old room into my mother's art studio so she didn't have to work in the basement, and they turned my sister's childhood bedroom into the guest room.

So, yeah, my mother paints erotic pictures in my old bedroom, and she's now decided to display them in Mackenzie's old room.

How fun.

I can't help wishing my parents were normal, but I suppose nobody thinks their parents are normal, do they?

"Yes, it was necessary!" Mom says. "There's no more space in our bedroom."

"Of course there isn't."

"Don't be such a prude, Peter! The naked female form is a lovely thing."

I immediately think of Valerie.

"But you're my mother," I say. "I don't need to fall asleep next to one of your vagina paintings."

"Oh, it's not a vagina, it's—"

"Mom, no! I don't need to hear the details. I'll see it soon enough."

She laughs. "Speaking of lady parts, how is this new girlfriend of yours? She's welcome to stay here while we're gone, we don't mind."

"She might be too scandalized by your paintings."

"Nonsense!"

We speak for a few more minutes before I put down the phone, shaking my head. Sometimes my parents are a little too much for me.

But then I look at the penguin card from Valerie.

Inside, she's written, *Thank you for being you.*

My mouth splits into a grin.

"So, how's it going with your fake girlfriend?" Leon asks.

Leon, Aaron and I are sitting in a sports bar in Thornhill, within walking distance of my parents' house.

"Oh, it's going great." I take a sip of my IPA.

Leon and Aaron look at each other.

"What?" I say.

"Have you slept together yet?" Leon asks.

"None of your business."

"So that means yes."

"None of your business."

"Have you bought her red roses?" Aaron asks. "A box of chocolates in the shape of a heart?"

"Now listen," I say. "You two are wrong about romance. You think it's all roses and chocolate and bubble baths." Well, actually, there was a bubble bath. A very enjoyable one. And we ate flourless chocolate cake together. But... "But it's really about getting to know a woman and giving her something special, just for her. Something no other guy would have gotten her."

"Thank you, Romeo," Leon says.

I roll my eyes. "And she's my real girlfriend now, just saying."

Aaron starts humming "Oops!...I Did It Again," something he picked up from Mackenzie several years back.

"You're going to tell us you've never felt like this before," Leon says, "aren't you?"

I open my mouth, then close it.

Yes, I've never felt like this before. It's true.

Isn't it?

"You say that every time," Aaron says.

"Well, not *every* time," Leon interjects, "but this would be far from the first."

"Not that there's anything wrong with liking relationships," Aaron continues. "It's not my cup of tea, but it's yours, and that's cool. It's just that you act like each one is different and special, then in six months to a year, you'll have broken up and be talking about a new woman."

"Now that's unfair." I have another sip of my beer. "I was single for eight months before Valerie."

Leon shrugs. "An aberration."

"I don't fall in love as easily as I did when I was younger."

But although my friends are annoying me, they might have a point.

How can I really know that what I have with Valerie is different from what I've had with other women? It hasn't been all that long yet—that's true.

"What do you think, girl?" I ask Biscuit when I take her for a walk later that evening. "Is Valerie special? Is she The One?"

Biscuit looks annoyed. *Shut your damn pie hole and pay attention to me!*

I don't think it's an Instagram-worthy look.

"Will her parents still like me when they discover I work in landscaping?"

Biscuit barks once, which I assume means, *Not likely.*

Well, I'll cross that bridge when we come to it, but for now I'm more concerned with the first question.

What Valerie and I have is great, and I've been smitten with her from the very beginning, but is it really different from what I've had before?

Chapter 18

Valerie

"How is it going with Peter?" Mom asks me on Friday night.

We're sitting in the living room together, in front of the TV, but we're not paying much attention to it.

"It's going well," I say.

"I worry, though. He's a pediatrician, and you work at an ice cream shop. Maybe it doesn't bother him now, but it will eventually. If you were a software developer, it would be better. More respectable. You should go back to your old career."

I tamp down my longing. "You know I can't do that."

"Aiyah! Why not? I am always hearing about how there are lots of opportunities for people who can program. Are you saying these are lies?"

"Mom, I—"

"You are experienced, too, and graduated second in your class."

I sigh. "You know I applied for jobs after I quit, but I couldn't get anything. Because I can't get a good reference from anyone at my old job. Because no one wants to hire a woman who accused her previous boss of sexual harassment—and when they ask why I left, I'm always honest about that part."

"Maybe you shouldn't be. Try again! Try harder!"

I shake my head. "I've accepted it. It's just not going to happen."

"Then start your own business."

"I'm not interested in that."

"Easier to find a job when you still have one. You should not have quit when you did."

I tense. "Do you really think I should have stayed after what happened?"

"Temporarily? Yes. I know what your boss did was wrong, but it might have been better for your career." She pauses. "I'm just afraid Peter will not stay with a woman who scoops ice cream for a living."

It's on the tip of my tongue to tell her that Peter isn't actually a doctor, but I hold it back.

The truth is, however, that a part of me *does* feel like he's too good for me. Not because of my job, but because he's so kind and sweet and easygoing, and I'm...difficult.

Yeah, I think that's how many people would describe me. Difficult.

Yet Peter bakes me muffins and buys me durian pancakes and goes down on me in the shower and arranges for me to have a day all to myself. Compared to how other men have treated me, this is a revelation. Some men are actually wonderful. Who would have guessed?

It seems too good to be true.

I push that thought aside.

But I'm still shaken by my conversation with my mom and the uncomfortable memories she's stirred up.

"What *is* that?" I ask, pointing at the painting on the wall across from us.

It's Sunday morning, and Peter and I are lying in the guest bed in his parents' house. I feel a little weird about being here when his parents are gone, but he assures me it's fine.

"It's my mom's latest painting," he says, "and everything my mom paints has something to do with the female form. Fortunately, this one is more abstract than usual, so I don't actually know what it is. Though she's assured me it's not a vagina."

"How comforting."

He laughs.

We woke up an hour ago and had leisurely sex, but I'm in no hurry to get up. When we're in bed together, it feels like we're in our own little world, even with his mother's painting on the wall.

"How about I bring you breakfast in bed?" Peter suggests.

Twenty minutes later, he sets a tray with coffee, an omelet, toast, and bacon in front of me. I'm still naked, and it feels weird to eat a meal when I'm not wearing any clothes. I start to pull on a shirt, but he stops me.

"You look good like this," he murmurs. "Stay."

"That hardly seems fair. You put clothes on to cook."

"Because I had a bad experience cooking in the nude."

I stifle a laugh. "What happened?"

"I was making breakfast for a girl, and the pan was hotter than I thought, and, well...oil splashed on my dick. It was painful, to say the least."

"Poor baby." I reach into his boxers and stroke his dick.

"Valerie," he groans. "Eat the food before it gets cold."

"What if I want to put something else in my mouth instead?"

Oh my God, who's the woman who's talking like this? It doesn't seem like me.

But I feel like I can say anything with Peter and it'll be okay.

I take my hand out of his boxers and begin eating.

He just stares at me.

"What?" I say around a mouthful of delicious cheese-and-mushroom omelet.

"I don't know how I'm supposed to eat when you're sitting there, looking like that, and you just had your hand down my pants."

"You're the one who wanted me to eat in the nude."

"I know, I know, you just look so…" He gestures toward me, as though he, the English major, lacks the vocabulary to describe my beauty.

"You'll manage." I hold a piece of omelet up to his lips with my fork, and he eats it.

He then takes the fork from me and feeds me a piece of omelet.

We lean toward each other, and just before his lips touch mine, there's a loud bark. We jump apart as though we've been caught doing something illicit.

"Biscuit!" Peter says to the fluffy white dog who trots into the room with her tongue hanging out of her mouth.

She barks again.

"Fine, fine, if you insist." He feeds her a tiny piece of cheese.

Oh my God, this man is adorable, and it feels so freaking domestic, lazing in bed together on a Sunday morning, with breakfast and a dog.

My heart clenches.

I swore off serious relationships after what happened with Stephen, but now I'm in a relationship again, and I want this kind of future with Peter. I can't help it.

I want to live with him. I want to buy a house together. I even want the freaking puppy who's so cute she almost looks fake.

The realization of how much I want this scares me.

And Peter, because he notices everything, says, "You okay, Valerie?"

"Yeah. Totally okay."

I smile and try not to think too much about the future.

Peter has promised to drop me off at Ginger Scoops around eleven thirty, which means we need to leave at eleven. But at ten o'clock, he says we should leave early because he has a surprise for me.

His last surprise was taking me to Doctor Durian, and I doubt anything could top that, but I'm sure it'll be good.

We get in the car with Biscuit. Apparently, the dog is coming with us. Less than half an hour later, we pull up to a park in midtown.

"Sherwood Park," he says. "You been here before?"

I shake my head.

We start walking, Peter holding Biscuit's leash. At first, the park seems like nothing special, but then we enter a forested area, and...oh my God.

It's the middle of October, and there's still a little green, but the leaves are mostly golden, with some orange and red maples.

"It's an off-leash dog area." Peter reaches down to unclasp Biscuit's leash.

She runs happily ahead of us, and Peter takes my hand. We walk in silence for a few minutes, leaves crunching underfoot. It's a sunny fall day with blue skies, but there's a brisk wind. In my trench coat, I'm just barely warm enough, but with Peter by my side, I don't care about the wind.

"I thought the leaves would be at their peak this weekend," he says. "And I was right. Let me take a picture of you."

We step onto a wooden boardwalk, and he takes a couple of pictures of me with the leaves, then insists on taking one of the two of us, which I grudgingly allow.

He makes it the background on his phone.

Then he says, "I need to take a picture of Biscuit for her Instagram account."

"I still can't believe your parents have an Instagram account for their dog."

I looked at it the other night. There were pictures of Biscuit looking cute in various different settings. To be honest, I found it a little repetitive, but she does have lots of fans.

Peter takes a photo of Biscuit, and then he asks me to take one of him with Biscuit.

My heart should not be melting like this. I should not be swept away by cute dogs and hot men, either separately or in combination.

Except this romantic walk in the park is certainly getting to me.

Breakfast in bed certainly got to me.

Somehow, Peter is taking apart the wall I built around myself, brick by brick, and I feel vulnerable.

"You know what my mom said the other day?" I don't wait for him to answer. I need to start putting some of those bricks back in place. "She said I wasn't good enough for you—"

"Your own mother said that?"

"Well, she didn't use those exact words. But she can't see how a doctor would want to date someone who works in an ice cream shop, at least not in the long term."

"Valerie." He stops and puts his hands on my shoulders. "I like you for exactly who you are. Even if I were a real doctor, I'd feel the same way. You're brilliant and beautiful."

"Brilliant." I snort. What could I have possibly done to make him think that?

He gives me a look. "I mean it."

And then he kisses me. He winds his arms around my body and presses his lips to mine, and it's bliss. There are many layers of clothing between us, but I can still feel the warmth of him, his heart beating against my chest.

It's wonderful. It's perfect. Everything he does is just what I need.

It scares me.

Because I'm falling in love with him, and nothing this wonderful can last.

I try to smile at the little girl with pigtails as I hand over her ice cream cone, but I can't seem to manage it. I'm not in a great mood.

It's been two hours since Peter dropped me off at Ginger Scoops, and I've been grumpy ever since.

It's too good to be true.

You know what happened the last time you fell in love. You're an idiot.

Is everyone else's self-talk this annoying, or is it just mine?

I remind myself of all the ways Peter is unlike Stephen. For example, Peter is not personally insulted that I want to use a vibrator in the bedroom. Peter makes me breakfast and respects my need for time alone.

But surely everything was good at the beginning with Stephen, right? It's just hard to remember when all I can think of is the end.

I can't imagine Peter acting the way my ex did, but I haven't known him for long enough to say that for sure, have I? I have lots of experience with men treating me well for a long time before showing their true colors. Why should I think Peter is any different?

He just is. There are good men in the world.

But why would one of those good men want to be with a failed software developer who isn't exactly good-natured? Those men don't go for women like you.

My mind is at war with itself.

A couple comes in with three kids, including a toddler who's screaming her head off, and oh my God, I can't deal with this right now.

Partly because when I look at these kids, I imagine Peter and me with our own kids. The thought is not unpleasant, and that scares the crap out of me.

I can't wait until this day is over.

"How's it going with your fake boyfriend?" Sarah asks.

Sarah, Chloe and I are having bubble tea after finishing work on Sunday. The tea shop is called The Lodge, and Chloe described its décor as "Canadian hipster," which I think is appropriate. The place is somewhat reminiscent of a hunting lodge, and their logo is a moose. The servers are wearing flannel.

Frankly, I think it's pretentious as shit, but my genmaicha latte with tapioca is good.

"Peter is great," I say, "and it's not fake anymore."

Chloe sips her tea. "You don't sound enthusiastic."

"It's too good to be true!" I blurt out.

"Nah, you just found a good guy. You think you can't have what Drew and I have? What Josh and Sarah have?"

"Well…no."

"Why not?" Sarah asks.

"Because you two are nice! I'm not."

Chloe chuckles. "Yes, you are."

"You know what I mean."

"Val, why do you think we've been friends for so long? We wouldn't be friends if I didn't like you. Why don't you think Peter can feel the same way?"

"You know why."

Chloe knows the whole story, though Sarah doesn't. It happened before I met her, and I haven't felt like filling her in on the details. I want to talk about it as little as possible.

"I understand why you think this way," Chloe says slowly, "but please don't throw this away. When you're not worrying that it's too good to be true, you seem happy, and he treats you better than Stephen ever did, even at the beginning."

"Do you think?"

She nods.

But when I started going out with Stephen, it was soon after Chloe's mother died, and I'm not convinced Chloe truly remembers.

"It can't last," I say. "It just can't."

"Don't think about the future," Sarah says. "Just enjoy it for now and see where it takes you."

"Last time I was caught off-guard because I hadn't been paying attention. I'm not making that mistake again. I have my eyes wide open. And I can't help thinking that there must be something more to Peter, something he's not telling me."

I have another sip of my genmaicha latte and suck a tapioca pearl up through the thick straw. The roasted brown rice in genmaicha gives it a unique flavor, and I've always liked it.

"I can believe in love for other people," I say quietly, "just not for me."

Chloe reaches across the table and squeezes my hand. "Valerie."

I shake my head. I don't want to talk about this anymore.

"You know what we should do?" Chloe says, upbeat. "We should have a triple date."

"Yes!" Sarah says. "Wouldn't that be fun? I'm dying to meet Peter."

"And I haven't spent much time with him, either," Chloe says. "We can get to know him a little better and give him our opinion. What do you think?"

"Alright." It does sound rather fun, I admit. "Maybe on Friday?"

"Pretty sure Drew has no plans," Chloe says.

"I'll check with Josh," Sarah says. "Then I'll come up with a restaurant and make reservations."

The conversation turns to our pie à la mode specials, which are served both at Ginger Scoops and Happy as Pie on Saturdays. Sarah and Chloe debate whether serving the pear ginger crumble pie with ginger ice cream would be too gingery, and, of course, they decide they have to try it first.

I smile and laugh, and I roll my eyes at the hipster-ness of the bubble tea shop and imagine bringing Peter here. We'd have a good time together, as we always do.

Okay, for now, I will try not to worry about where this is going.

But I suspect it will be impossible to banish my fears completely.

Chapter 19

Peter

Valerie looks gorgeous tonight. She's wearing a red shirt and tight dark jeans, and when she laughs at something her friend Sarah says, it makes me grin.

We're on a triple date with two of her friends and their boyfriends, at a restaurant in North York. It specializes in food from one of the northern Chinese provinces, and there's lots of lamb on the menu. Josh and Sarah ordered for the table, and now we're waiting for our food to arrive.

"So, what do you do?" I ask Josh.

Sarah laughs and puts a hand on his shoulder. "Josh is a CEO."

I raise my eyebrows. "Oh?"

I rarely feel insecure about what I do for a living. I make okay money, and I don't mind the work. It suits me.

But Valerie's friend is apparently dating a CEO, and that makes me feel just a touch...

Insecure, yeah.

Josh doesn't fit my image of a CEO. For one, I always imagine them wearing suits, but I suppose even important people can take a little time off, in between making lots of money and ordering people around.

"You seem a little young for that," I say. I'd guess he's a few years older than me, but not much.

He shrugs. "We do mobile app development and custom software."

Now he's piqued my interest. "You must have a bunch of software developers working for you."

"Of course."

I swing my gaze to Valerie, who shifts uncomfortably in her seat. I desperately want to know what pushed her away from her career, but now is not the time.

"How did you two meet?" I ask Josh and Sarah.

Sarah turns a little pink. "He, um, came into my shop one day, and he liked my pies. No, that's not innuendo. Later, he asked me to cater a Pi Day party for him, and that's how we started spending time together."

"Cool." I like hearing people's how-we-met stories. They're always fun. "You know, I went to a friend's wedding in the summer, and he had a pie buffet. I think it was done by Happy as Pie."

"Was this Caitlin and Wes's wedding?"

"Yes! Wes and I play hockey together."

"You play hockey?" Valerie asks.

"For fun, yeah. I'm not that great. But it's taught me just how badly hockey equipment can stink, and that's still a hell of a lot better than durian." I wink at her.

"I'm told that's how you met," Josh says. "You weren't watching where you were going, and you ran into Valerie when she was carrying a durian ice cream cone."

"That's right," Valerie says.

"Hold on a second," I say. "You've got this wrong. Yes, I wasn't paying attention because I was looking at my phone. My dad had just texted me to ask if I'd been to a nudist beach, because he and my mom wanted to go."

"Your parents went to a nudist beach?" Josh asks in surprise.

"Shh. The less said about that, the better. Though it's perhaps less disturbing than the fact that my mother occasionally poses nude for art classes."

"Your mom poses nude?" Valerie splutters.

"So I'm told."

"Good for her," Chloe says. "For being comfortable with her body."

"Yeah, it's great. Just wonderful. If she weren't my *mother*." Josh howls.

"Back to our how-we-met story," I say. "I was standing on the patio—and true, I was kind of in the way—but Valerie wasn't looking where she was going, and she barged into me. Of course, since I had durian ice cream on me, I took off my shirt—"

"Only sensible," Josh murmurs.

"—and she invited me into Ginger Scoops to get cleaned up, and then she gave me free ice cream and asked if I wanted to be her fake boyfriend."

"Yes," Valerie says, "it went something like that."

"What about you two?" I turn to Chloe.

"Oh, Drew would take his niece into Ginger Scoops. He was hard to forget because he always ordered black coffee and talked about how he hated ice cream."

"Are you lactose intolerant?" I ask.

"No," he says. "My ex wrote that *Embrace Your Inner Ice Cream Sandwich* book, and it turned me off ice cream."

"You're dating a woman who owns an ice cream shop, and you hate ice cream?"

"Hated. Past tense," Chloe clarifies. "He likes it now."

The lamb skewers arrive. Valerie eagerly picks one up and starts eating the lamb off the metal skewer, and I'm so mesmerized by her mouth that I almost forget to eat my own food.

But eventually I do, and it is indeed delicious and juicy.

More food arrives. Fried cumin lamb with peppers and onions, hand-pulled noodles with lamb, two types of dumplings, fried lamb pancakes, braised eggplant, and some kind of crispy beef.

I must say, Josh and Sarah did a good job ordering.

And Valerie does a good job of slurping noodles in a way that makes me want to use her mouth for other purposes. We're sitting across from each other, and I lean forward to put my hand on her thigh under the table.

I like spending time with Valerie's friends, but I can't wait to get her alone and take off that little red shirt. Sure, I might not be a big success like Josh, but I can give her what she needs and deserves.

I frown as I remember the questions Aaron and Leon raised, then push them aside and focus on my girlfriend once more. I'm simply going to be here in this moment with her and enjoy it for all that it is.

When we get to my parents' house after dinner, Biscuit runs up to me and barks. I take her out for a few minutes, and then, at last, it's Valerie and me, all alone.

I hoist her up in my arms and carry her to the guest bedroom. Immediately, I set to work on her clothes. I pull off her shirt, which looks great on her, but it looks even better on the floor. I unclasp her bra to reveal her breasts, their peaks standing at attention. She squirms.

God, I love seeing how she needs me.

I rub my erection against her through our jeans, and she squirms even more. Then she removes my shirt and jeans.

"In a rush for something?" I ask.

I roll onto my side as she slips her hand inside my boxers, and I hiss out a breath when she touches me. Her lower lip is trembling; I suck it between my teeth.

I love how responsive she is.

I slide my hand inside her panties and run my finger along her slit. "I'm gonna fuck you real good tonight," I say. "Real good."

The first time we did it, we talked more, so I could understand what she needed. She was embarrassed about what she needed to come, but it didn't bother me. Everyone requires something a little different. All I want is to please her in bed, however that might happen, and I think I'm doing a pretty good job.

Maybe someday, I'll find a way to bring her to orgasm without a vibrator, and I'm happy to spend lots of time trying. But the last thing she needs is pressure, especially with a new guy.

Once I tear off the rest of our clothes, I roll on top of her. I press the length of my naked body along hers; that always makes her whimper in pleasure. When I slip my hand between her legs again, she's wet for me, and I fucking love it. I push my finger into her a few times and curl it upwards, and she takes hold of my cock and pumps up and down.

Just touching each other like this—it's amazing. Her hand wrapped around me...

Dear God.

I slide my finger into my mouth to taste her, and her eyes widen. I lick my thumb before moving it back between her legs, fingering her as I rub her clit.

One of the things I've learned about her? She loves being fingered like this.

She lets go of my cock so she can clutch the sheets, and she squeezes her eyes shut.

I kiss her. I have to kiss her, this woman who is unraveling beneath me. When I lick her bottom lip, she opens for me, lets my tongue tangle with hers as I stroke her.

"Yes," she groans against my mouth.

I slide down the bed so my mouth is between her legs, and I continue to stroke my finger in and out of her as I lick over her entrance and up to her clit. She bucks her hips against me, and I smile, my face buried in her pussy. I add a second finger, and she grabs a handful of my hair and holds me there between her legs.

As if I would go anywhere.

I continue to lick her, reveling in her taste, her reaction. I slide a hand lower and pump my cock a few times.

"Peter," she whispers, and I look up.

I know what she wants. I grab the vibrator that she placed at the edge of the bed earlier, and I turn it on and press it to her clit. I lie next to her on my side, stroking her hair and kissing her as I watch the tension build in her body. Her fists are practically as white as the sheets, and her back bows off the bed as she's overcome with her climax.

She screams, as always.

I fucking love it when she screams.

She told me she never has the urge to scream when she's alone, and she seemed surprised that it always happens when she's with me.

I can't lie; it makes me feel damn good.

"How was that, baby?" I murmur, kissing her hair and setting aside the vibrator. "You ready for me to fuck you?"

She nods vigorously.

She might swear a lot, but she seems uncomfortable talking dirty in bed—and that's cool. She enjoys when I do it on occasion, though.

I roll on a condom in a hurry, but not so much of a hurry that I forget to add lube. When I push inside her, she's still shuddering from her orgasm.

My God.

She feels amazing.

I undulate my hips in a steady rhythm, and I kiss her. Oh, how I kiss her.

She kisses me back eagerly, her mouth so sweet against my own, and this, I think, is heaven. I don't see how it could get any better than this.

But then her pussy clenches around my cock.

"Valerie," I growl.

She tilts her hips toward mine and wraps her legs around me, pushing up to meet me again and again. I take one of her nipples into my mouth and feast on it as we move in unison. Being with her is overwhelming.

And I want her to come for me again.

I grab the vibrator, turn it on, and press it to her clit as I push inside her, trying my best to use it just the way she showed me, but it's hard to think straight, overwhelmed as I am with the sensation of having her around me and underneath me.

But a moment later, she comes apart. I press my mouth to hers and swallow her scream...and I finish inside her before collapsing on my back.

She cuddles up against me afterward. "Mm. That was so good. I feel like jelly. Like I don't have bones anymore."

"That's quite a disturbing condition. I think it merits further investigation." I slide my hand down her leg and tap her knee. "Hmm. Feels okay to me."

She laughs.

"Can you come more than twice?" I ask.

"Actually, today is the first time I've ever had multiple orgasms. It's only happened with you."

"If you keep this up, I'm going to have an inflated ego."

"Perhaps I should examine your ego."

For some reason, this involves studying my abs. She presses on them and scrapes her fingers over them. "Seems okay to me. No signs of swelling."

"You make a great doctor, darling."

"So do you."

She kisses my cheek, then rolls to the left side of the bed—her side—and falls asleep. I brush my hand over her arm, thinking that there's nowhere else in the universe I'd rather be.

Soon, I join her in slumber.

Chapter 20

Peter

Saturday morning, I wake up to Valerie nuzzling my nose.

Although she prefers that we sleep on separate sides of the bed, once she's awake, she'll shift over to my side and snuggle up against me. We've spent the night together a few times so far, and even though it hasn't been long, I know this will never get old.

"Hey, Val," I say, my eyes still closed.

Wait a second. Valerie smells kind of funny. And why is her nose wet?

I crack open an eye.

It's Biscuit.

The dog wags her tail when I sit up. I glance at the other side of the bed, where Valerie is lying, her breathing telling me that she's still asleep.

I sigh. "Alright, Biscuit. I'll take you outside. Just give me a minute to get dressed."

Biscuit and I head downstairs, and after she does her business outside, I take a short video of her and post it on Instagram.

When I get back upstairs, Valerie is on her back, stretching her hands above her head.

I shed my clothes in a flash and climb back in with her, curling my body around hers. It's eight o'clock, so we still have time before she has to get ready for work.

"Good morning," I say.

"Morning." Her voice is heavy with sleep.

We stay in bed together for a while, idly touching each other here and there. I close my eyes, but sleep doesn't overtake me; I just enjoy this moment with her. Her body pressed against mine is perfection.

"I'm a bit sore from last night," she says.

I immediately prop up my head and look at her. "Was I too rough?"

"No, I enjoyed every second of it. I guess my body is still getting used to having sex again. And two orgasms in ten minutes!" She laughs, delighted, as though she still can't believe this. "I'd never used a vibrator during penetration before, which means I hadn't come while a guy was inside me. Until last night."

"You and Stephen didn't try it?" That seems like an obvious thing to do, considering she needs it to orgasm.

"I know! It's ridiculous. But he didn't..." She shakes her head.

"You guys were together a long time, weren't you?"

"Four years."

I hesitate. "What happened, exactly?"

She's silent for a minute.

"You don't have to tell me," I say hurriedly. "It's okay. I was just curious." I do, desperately, want to know, but if she's not ready, I can wait.

"No, it's fine. I don't like talking about it, but I want you to know what happened with Stephen and my career." She rolls onto her side, facing me. "Stephen Shum and I met in undergrad. We were in the same program, and he'd developed an app in high school and was still making money off it...and, well, I kind of idolized him. He didn't notice me, though, not until fourth year. That's when we started dating. I'd only dated one guy before him, but it hadn't lasted long. Anyway, we graduated, managed to get decent jobs in our field, and moved in together. None of our parents were thrilled with that part, but Mom liked him. He was respectable. Good Chinese family." She's quiet for a moment. "I was happy. I had a job as a software developer at a small engineering software company, the place where I'd worked the previous summer. Stephen had a job at a larger firm, but he didn't plan to stay long term. He had a couple of other apps he was developing on the side. I didn't work on the code, but I would give him advice on the UX/UI."

"What's that?" I ask.

"User experience, user interface. He didn't always have a great sense for that stuff, but I did." She absently runs her finger along my arm. "My boss had had a bunch of summer students before, but he didn't have great things to say about them. But me...he thought I was really smart. He respected my opinions. When I started working there full-time, I told him about all the ideas I had to make the software more user-friendly, and he let me implement most of the changes I wanted."

She's jumping between her relationship and her job, and I don't quite get how it all fits together, but I think she needs to tell the story her way.

"I liked that job," Valerie says. "Even when I wasn't at work, I was always thinking about it. How to solve problems, how to make it better. I felt lucky that I'd been able to graduate from university and get a job in my field right away—not everyone has that chance. And I was good at it. I know you have nothing to go on but my word, but I was."

"I believe you," I say. "You don't seem like the type to exaggerate your abilities."

She snorts. "Yeah, I'm not a man. Anyway, the job was good, my relationship with Stephen... Well, it wasn't always the greatest, and he thought I was a bit of a frigid bitch in the bedroom."

"*What?*"

She smiles wanly. "Because I didn't get as wet as some women, and because I didn't have enough screaming orgasms."

"You have plenty with me."

"Because you're not insecure enough to be threatened by a vibrator. I suggested we use toys, but Stephen didn't like the idea. And he didn't realize that I could only orgasm with a vibrator, because occasionally I would fake it, just so he would feel better." She shakes her head. "I know it's weird to tell you about this. I'm actually trying to pay you a compliment—sex with you is the best I've ever had." She gives me a shy smile, then looks down.

Feeling like this is the time for a little levity, I press on my stomach. "No swelling. I guess your compliments didn't get to my head...or my abs."

She laughs. "So it wasn't great between Stephen and me, but I wasn't paying enough attention to how bad it actually was, and I thought that was just the way relationships were. I didn't have much experience."

Ugh. I hate this guy. He sounds like a tool.

"Now back to my job," she says. "I used to help my boss do training sessions for engineers. I liked to see what was intuitive and what was difficult for new users. It wasn't something that I was initially hired to do, but I enjoyed it on occasion. Anyway, my boss and I were in Calgary for a few days, running a training session, and..." She swallows. "We were having dinner, and we'd each had a glass of wine, but we weren't drunk. And he made a pass at me."

"That fucker," I mutter, clenching my fist. I'm not usually quick to anger, but Valerie's story is making it hard for me to control my emotions.

I do my best, though. This is about her, not me.

"It's common." She's trying to detach herself, but her voice is wavering. "I tried to laugh it off, but he kept going. He put his hand on my leg and told me no one would have to know, not my boyfriend or his wife, it would be our secret."

I run my hands through Valerie's hair, trying to give her strength however I can.

"I was horrified," she says. "Shocked. I know it's not uncommon for women to experience this sort of thing in the workplace, but I never had, and he'd always treated me well, never made any mention of this. Although once or twice, I'd thought he'd looked at me funny, then shrugged it off as my imagination—now I know it wasn't. I thought of him as a father figure. When he put his hand on my leg, I was so disgusted. I told him never to do it again."

She pauses to take a breath, and I hold her close, wishing I could make it all go away.

"Afterward, I fled to my hotel room," she continues, "but despite what I'd said, the next morning, he tried again. I said I was his employee and this was sexual harassment, but he acted like I owed him. Not knowing what else to do, I finished the training session with him. When I returned to Toronto, I told Chloe, no one else. I was scared that if I told Stephen, he would accuse me of sending signals to my boss, saying it wouldn't have happened otherwise."

I've never hated anyone so much in my life.

"So, I talked to Chloe and decided to quit. As much as I liked the job, I couldn't stand to be there a day longer, and I started to wonder if maybe I wasn't all that smart, and my boss had just been trying to get in my pants the whole time. And I think the whole #metoo thing empowered me to speak up, made me feel like I wasn't alone."

"Why didn't you go to HR?"

She laughs without humor. "It was a small company. There was my boss...and everyone else. There was no HR. Plus, I think HR is mainly about looking out for the interests of the company, not necessarily the employees. Anyway, the day I quit, it was one of Those Days. The day you might see in a book or movie, when a woman loses her boyfriend, her job, and her apartment all in one shot. After quitting my job, I got home early and found Stephen in bed with another woman."

"I'm so sorry you had to go through all this," I say, an intense pain in my heart.

"Oh, just you wait. It gets worse. Not when it comes to Stephen—I dumped his ass right away. But when it comes to work." She pauses. "I moved back home and immediately started applying for jobs. I was determined not to let this get me down. I got a few interviews, and a couple of them seemed impressed with me. I expected to get an offer, and then...nothing.

"Finally, I got a phone call from a woman who worked for one of these companies. She told me she wasn't supposed to be making this call, but she wanted me to know why I didn't get the job. The problem was my reference. I couldn't use my old boss as a reference, of course, so I used another software developer at my old company, one who'd been a mentor of sorts to me. I'd told him why I quit, and I trusted him. But apparently he was telling my prospective employers that I'd made a false accusation of sexual harassment against my boss and was not to be trusted, and of course nobody wants to hire someone who has a history of making false accusations of sexual harassment. The woman was so sorry, she'd fought for me, she believed me, but she was the most junior person on the hiring committee." Tears shimmer in Valerie's eyes. "My career was stolen from me."

She lets out a choked sob, and I pull her against my chest and hold her tight.

"Men are bastards," I say, my voice vibrating with anger.

"Such bastards," she agrees. "So when Chloe told me she was going to open an ice cream parlor, I jumped at the chance to work with her. I wanted to get far away from what I'd been doing before, and I knew I wouldn't have to deal with sexual harassment from my new boss, which was a step up. And here I am." She sighs and snuggles up closer to me.

I open my mouth, then shut it again.

I want to fix this for her. Surely there must be something she can do, rather than giving up the career she loved.

But I don't think that's what she needs right at this moment, so I don't say anything.

The amount of rage I feel on her behalf is almost frightening. It's not a feeling I have experience much with, but I can't bear the thought of her going through this nightmare. My Valerie.

I try to unclench my jaw as I hold her tight. I kiss her hair, her wet cheeks, her neck.

"Distract me," she murmurs, taking my hand and putting it between her legs.

"You sure?"

"Yes. Make me forget."

I kiss my way down her body and use my fingers to part her folds. She's not very wet, so I squeeze some lube on my finger before I slip it inside her. She gasps.

"Tell me if I do something you don't like, or if you want something I'm not doing, okay?"

She nods.

I lie next to her and kiss her leisurely as I stroke my finger in and out of her body. She's in my arms, and she's mine. Despite all the crap that has happened to her before, she's begun to trust me, and that's something she doesn't do easily.

And now, I know why.

I run my fingers up and down her slit before pushing two fingers inside her. Her moisture might not be dripping down her thighs, but after a few minutes of playing with her, she's pretty wet, and I love it.

"You said you don't get very wet, but you do," I say. "Not the first time or two, but you do now."

I think it took her a while to feel completely comfortable being intimate with me, and her ex was a total bastard, so she probably never felt like this with him.

"Mm, maybe you're right," she says, her voice heavy with desire.

I slide down her body and run my tongue over her. She tastes so fucking good. My cock is hard, but I try not to focus on that. This is about Valerie.

I slip my fingers in and out of her as I run my tongue over her clit. She clenches the blankets in her fists and her breaths become quicker. She's getting there, but I know she won't get all the way there without the vibrator. I grab it from the bedside table and turn it on, and only seconds after I press it to her clit, she screams out for me. "*Peter.*"

I turn off the vibrator and crawl up the bed. "You want another one?"

She shakes her head, and then she grasps my cock. I hiss out a breath. "I'm sorry, I'm sore inside, I can't—"

"Don't apologize," I say. She's got her hand wrapped around my cock. There's no need for an apology.

She strokes my erection between us as we kiss. Pumping up and down, increasing her speed a little.

Fuck. "Val, I'm going to…"

I come all over her hand, but she's not bothered by the mess.

"Maybe we could get a smaller vibrator," I say a few minutes later. "A U-shaped one that could be worn during sex. What do you think?"

"Maybe, but…" Her face turns a pretty shade of pink. "I don't want to go to a sex store again. It was bad enough the first time. The saleslady asked if I needed help, and I was mortified."

"You can order online."

"And have it shipped to my parents' house? My mother would open it. She has no sense of boundaries."

"No, we'll ship it to my place." I press a kiss to her cheek. "We'll look at some things online, you tell me what you'd like, and I'll get it for us, okay? I'll take care of it."

"Thank you," she says, as though it's more than just a little thing.

I press another kiss to her face. "Now how about we shower together and get cleaned up?"

After our very enjoyable shower, we go downstairs for breakfast, and I decide this is the day for the little treat I've stashed in my parents' freezer.

When I take out the package, Valerie's smile lights up her face.

This might stink up the kitchen, but I don't care. It's worth it.

I was at an Asian supermarket the other day, and I found myself looking at something I'd never looked at before: frozen durian. They sell the whole ones frozen, but I don't think Valerie needs a whole durian for herself, plus then I'd have to figure out how to hack it open. With a meat cleaver? An ax? I don't know.

But they also sold frozen durian in packages, so I got a small one.

"Maybe you could make a smoothie with it," I suggest.

I looked up recipes. Some had condensed milk, so I bought that for her, too, as well as some bananas, since I thought that might taste good.

Taste good to her, that is.

"No, I like to eat half-frozen durian just as it is. With a spoon. It's like frozen custard." She's practically salivating. "It's not too warm outside, but it's sunny—I'll put the package on the picnic table in the backyard for an hour, then eat it. You can have some, too." She winks at me.

"Not a chance."

We have a leisurely breakfast of cereal and coffee and oranges, and occasionally Valerie's voice wavers, like she's still recovering from what she told me, and I do my best to make her laugh and shower her with affection.

"I have lots of new Instagram followers," I tell her. "After I posted that picture of me and Biscuit on her account, everyone wondered who the 'handsome guy' was, and I linked to my own account."

"I hope I don't have any competition," Valerie says.

"Don't worry. I just want you."

"You know what you should do? Take sexy pictures of yourself with a durian and post them on Instagram. I'm sure they'd be popular."

"Hmm. For you, I'll consider it."

Eventually, her durian has defrosted enough to eat, and we put on our jackets and head outside with Biscuit. Valerie digs into her half-frozen durian with a spoon and sighs in bliss.

Biscuit barks. She's sitting on the ground, staring at Valerie's food.

"No, girl," I say, patting her head, "you don't want any of that. It's nasty stuff."

She barks again, not happy that I'm denying her something. *You're such an asshole. I am the supreme ruler of this household!*

It's always fun to imagine what Biscuit is thinking.

Valerie holds a small piece of durian in front of the dog's nose, and to my surprise, Biscuit is doesn't turn her head away in disgust at the smell of natural gas mixed with hockey equipment.

Indeed, after Valerie feeds her the small piece of half-frozen durian, Biscuit barks happily, her tongue poking out of her mouth.

"See?" Valerie says. "She has good taste. Unlike you."

"Very funny," I say as Biscuit wags her tail and jumps in my lap.

"I'm not going to feed her any more, though. I'm not sure how good durian is for dogs, plus I want to eat it all myself." Valerie shifts the package close to her, as if I would steal it.

Ha.

But you know what? Watching my not-so-fake girlfriend eat durian in the autumn sunshine while my parents' Instagram-star Bichon Frise lounges in my lap...it's kind of a perfect moment. A couple of months ago, I could never have imagined getting pleasure out of a situation that involved durian, but now, things are different.

I love her.

But I can't tell her, not yet. I wish I could, but I know she's not ready to hear it.

"I really like you," I say instead, placing my hand on top of Valerie's.

The words seem insufficient, but they'll have to do for now.

·❤·❤·❤·❤·❤·

Once Valerie leaves for work and I'm no longer trying to distract her, my fury on her behalf returns.

I decide to go for a run.

At first, I try going with Biscuit, but after a block, I discover she can't keep up and really isn't that great of a running companion, so I take her back to the house and set out on my own, just me and my thoughts about Valerie's ex and her boss and the colleague she used as a reference. All the men in her life who were complete shits to her.

She loved that career, and she was good at it. Not that I know anything about software development, but I believe her. I'm sure she's brilliant.

And I have to give it back to her.

She wanted a little distance from it at first, and after all that happened, I understand. But she needs that challenge now; she needs to create something. She hates having a job that involves dealing with people all day.

I know the lack of references is an issue, but surely there's something she can do. Couldn't she be self-employed? Or...I know!

Her friend's boyfriend, whom I met last night. Josh. He could hire her, or at least give her some advice on what she could do.

Today isn't the right time to bring it up, but I'll do it soon. I hate to see her living a life that isn't right for her, and hopefully, with my support, she can figure out how to make this work.

I will be with her every step of the way.

I will help her change her life.

And I can't help feeling that this is what I'm meant to do with *my* life.

Aaron and Leon were wrong. Sure, maybe I've said "I've never felt like this before" with other women, but in my vast experience with romance, it's never been quite like this for me. I'm older now, and I've had more relationships; I know what I'm talking about, unlike five or ten years ago.

And I just know that Valerie and I belong together. There's no other way to describe it.

I hope that soon, she'll be able to see it, too.

Chapter 21

Valerie

Tuesday—which is now part of my weekend!—my brother wants to meet me for lunch at the poke bowl place in Baldwin Village. We sit across from each other, me with my squid bowl and him with his salmon bowl, and for some reason, conversation isn't easy between us. Usually, Alan and I get along well, but today, it feels awkward.

Or maybe it's not him...it's just me.

I can't get Peter out of my mind.

Specifically, I can't get the conviction that there must be something *wrong* with Peter out of my mind. I banished my fears for a little while after that conversation with my friends—and my friends assured me, after our triple date, that Peter is great—but now, those fears have returned.

When I was telling Peter about what happened last year, a part of me couldn't help feeling like surely, this would be the end. He wouldn't believe me, or he'd say I should have stayed at my job until I found a new one, or he'd wonder if maybe I was encouraging my boss, and that's why he made a pass at me.

But Peter did none of those things.

The other option was that he would have been overcome with anger and demand I tell him where to find Stephen so he could beat the shit out of him, and when I refused, I'd have to spend an hour calming him down, as though he were the victim, not me.

But he didn't do that, either.

He was simply supportive. He listened. He didn't push me. He was properly outraged, but still calm. When I asked him to help me forget, he did.

In other words, he was perfect.

Maybe I shouldn't be surprised. The things I feared—those would have been out of character for him.

Nobody's perfect, though, and men have a tendency to be complete tools.

There must be something wrong with Peter, some skeleton in his closet. But what?

I push that aside and try to focus on my brother, try to think of something to ask him. Unfortunately, his geochronology research bores me, though the basic concept is cool. I'm glad he's found something he loves, even if Mom complains and says, "What are you going to do with that degree? Help me if I have a sick rock in my garden? Better to be a real doctor than a rock doctor."

I chuckle at the memory, then have a bite of my food and turn to one of my regular topics of conversation with my brother.

Instruct-Ed.

"So," I say, "any of your students manage to change their quiz marks again?"

"Nah, I figured out how to stop that from happening. It was completely non-intuitive, however. It would never have occurred to me if one of the customer support people hadn't told me what to do, and they acted like it was just common sense."

I shake my head. "I can't believe a big company makes such awful software. If only I could…"

Alan puts down his chopsticks and leans forward. "If only you could get your hands on the code. I know. You say that every time. You always ask about the course management software and fantasize about fixing it."

"Maybe 'fantasize' is putting it a bit strongly—"

"I can't stand to see you doing this to yourself. You want to be a software developer again. So do it."

"It's not that simple."

"Yes, it is, if you want something badly enough. I hate to see you wasting your life on scooping ice cream."

"Stop being a snob." I stab at a cherry tomato. "It's an honest day's work. Nothing wrong with that."

"But you're too smart for it."

"Such a snob." I shake my head again. "Is this why you wanted to see me for lunch? Just so you could critique my life choices? You sound like Mom."

"It's frustrating to see how all your confidence was stolen. You think your boss had ulterior motives whenever he complimented your work."

"I don't think that's unreasonable." It's true; that crushed some of my confidence. But I still have some conviction that I was good at what I did. I just don't know how I could stand it if that shit happened again. Alan thinks it was an aberration, but I've read so many #metoo stories. I know it's not uncommon.

And yes, I have to deal with some shitty behavior from customers at Ginger Scoops, but they're not in positions of power over me.

Plus, it's not that simple for me to get another job. I already tried.

"I'm not talking about this right now," I say.

He sighs. "Alright."

I eat my poke bowl in silence, hating that I feel uncomfortable with my own brother.

I go to Peter's after lunch. His parents are back from vacation, so they no longer need him to look after Biscuit, and Peter is living in his apartment once more. He's not home now, since he's at work, but he said I could relax here for a few hours.

I help myself to some of the smoked plum juice in his fridge before I start watching Netflix in peace and quiet. No mother to yell at me. No sister to argue with me. No father to...well, my dad doesn't say much, but he's always *there*.

At five o'clock, I hear the key in the door.

Peter is home!

I scurry to the door, and when he steps inside, I greet him by throwing my arms around him and kissing him on the lips.

"Hey, you," he says. "I could get used to coming home to this."

I smile back at him, even though I feel a twinge of discomfort. At his words, I can't help but think of being a housewife, and that was never what I wanted.

But, yeah, it's nice to be here to greet him after a day of work.

He showers while I make a pot of tea and take out the Japanese cheesecake I bought earlier. When he returns, he's wearing only a pair of pajama pants, his white T-shirt slung over his shoulder.

"That's an interesting way to wear a shirt," I say. "Normally one would make use of the arm and neck holes and not show off one's..." I gesture toward him.

"Show off my what?" he says with a smirk.

"Chest. Abs. Body in general."

"So glad you like my 'body in general.' That's a surprise."

Then he puts on his T-shirt and sits down at the counter with me. We eat our cheesecake in companionable silence for a minute, holding hands.

"Valerie," he says, "I want to help you get your career back. Whatever kind of support you need, I'm there. Have you considered going to a lawyer? I don't know exactly what they could do, but maybe—"

"I can't afford it, and I can't imagine going through that."

I nod. "I understand. What about asking Sarah's boyfriend—"

"No." I stiffen and think of my conversation with Alan. "I'm not going back to that world. Why would I want to work in an industry that did that to me?"

"But you loved it. Don't let them chase you out for good. You're going to do great things. I believe in you."

Well, I've finally figured out what's wrong with Peter So.

He believes in me!

The cheek of the man.

"I'm not asking Josh for a job." I push a little piece of cheesecake around on my plate. "Sarah suggested it, too, but I'm not going to take advantage of our friendship like that."

"People use their connections all the time in business. Obviously, you'll still have to do good work, and I know you will. Just ask. See what happens. If you were a rich white dude, you wouldn't hesitate."

Reluctantly, I chuckle.

He strokes my hand. "I just want you to do what makes you happy."

"I won't be happy. Maybe initially, but bad shit will happen."

"You don't trust Josh?"

"He's not the only person at the company."

Peter sighs. "Okay. I'll drop it for now. I know you went through something terrible."

And sure enough, he doesn't mention it again that day.

It's a bit of a relief to go back to Ginger Scoops on Thursday, to straighten the tables and put away the patio furniture, to make a banana split with green tea ice cream, chocolate-raspberry ice cream, and strawberry-lychee sorbet, as well as an excessive amount of chocolate sauce and sprinkles. It's a relief to make bubble waffles. It's a relief to wipe down the tables and mop the floor.

Ginger Scoops isn't my favorite place in the world—goddamn customers—but it's been a refuge of sorts for me, and I'm thankful to Chloe.

Alan and Peter just don't understand what it's like. Most men don't.

But Peter has been lovely. He tried his best today, even if he didn't fully get it, though I'm still convinced there must be something wrong with him.

Other than the fact that he believes in me and doesn't like durian, of course.

Chapter 22

Peter

"Remember when it smelled like natural gas here?" Carson asks as we move paper bags full of leaves to the curb. We're already up to fifty bags, and there are still lots of leaves to go.

This is what happens when it's fall and you have a property as big as Brian Poon's.

"How could I forget?" I mutter. "The man had hosted a party and served durian, and it smelled like goddamn rotten onions with a dash of sewage and body odor."

Carson regards me for a moment. "What's up with you, man? You're not your cheerful self today."

"Eh, just one of those days."

"Woman troubles. I bet that's what it is."

"I don't want to talk about it."

"Come on, buddy. It's me. We've worked together for years."

I swipe a hand through my hair. "I can take care of it."

I guess I am in a bad mood. Things are going well with Valerie...mostly. But I want her to pursue her dreams, and she won't. She's afraid. Though I understand why, I hate seeing her work at a job that doesn't give her satisfaction.

Now, I don't get any particular fulfilment from my own job, but it pays the bills and I don't mind it, and there isn't something else I'd rather be doing.

For Valerie, however, there definitely is.

I'll leave it for a few more days, but somehow, I have to change her mind.

I also can't help worrying that she'll never feel the same way about me as I feel about her. I tell myself to be patient, but it's hard.

When I arrive at my parents' house on Thursday after work, Biscuit immediately runs up to me, her tongue hanging out of her mouth and her tail wagging.

"Hey, girl," I say. "You glad to have Mommy and Daddy home again?"

"Smile!" says my father.

I look toward him and grin. He snaps a photo of me and Biscuit with his phone and, presumably, posts it on Instagram.

"You know," I say, "you could have said hello first."

He shrugs and holds out his arms

I embrace him. "How was your trip?"

"It was good."

Just then, I hear some yelling.

"No, I'm not wearing that!" Mackenzie shouts.

"Why not? You'll look good," Mom says.

"I can't wear it in public."

"I know. It's for you to wear with Benny."

"His name is Ben, not Benny."

I walk toward the living room, Biscuit on my heels, and see my mother and my sister.

Mackenzie gestures with her hand. She's holding some kind of black lacy fabric. "Can't you understand how weird this is?"

"What's going on?" I ask.

Mackenzie turns to me. "Mom bought me lingerie in Spain. Sexy lingerie. To wear when I'm…" She throws up her arms in the air. "Why can't you be a *normal* mother? One who doesn't paint pictures of vaginas and buy me sexy lingerie to wear with my boyfriend?"

"Okay, that's weird," I agree.

"You're lucky she didn't buy you any sexy lingerie."

"Actually…" Mom says.

I whip my head toward my mother. "Excuse me?"

"Just kidding. But you should see your face. No, we got you some orange wine."

I picture myself enjoying it with Valerie. "Excellent. That's a vast improvement."

"How come he gets wine and I get creepy lingerie?" Mackenzie asks.

"We got you wine, too," Dad says.

So my sister got two presents and I only got one.

That's okay. I think I came out ahead.

"I've never seen anything like it in Canada," Mom says, pointing at the black lace. "See here how it—"

"No!" Mackenzie howls, covering her ears with her hands.

Yeah, okay, I'm a grown man, and I probably shouldn't enjoy my sister's pain, but it does bring me a tiny bit of satisfaction. I can't help it.

"There's something called the internet," Mackenzie says. "I can order anything I want, from places all over the world. You don't need to get such things for me. The only person who can buy me lingerie without it being weird is Ben."

"*Does* he buy you lingerie?"

"It's none of your goddamn business!"

My mother laughs. She enjoys needling us way too much.

Dad turns to me. "Peter, we need to have a conversation about the package you left in the garbage while you were here."

I try to remain calm, but inside, I'm freaking out. What the hell is this about? Did I get careless with a condom wrapper?

"The frozen durian packaging," Dad clarifies.

Oh, thank God. That's all it was.

"I thought you hated durian." Mackenzie folds her arms over her chest.

"I do."

"The thing is," Dad says, "it kinda smelled."

"I'm sorry. I meant to take out the garbage, and then I forgot."

"Why did you buy durian if you hate it?" Mom asks. "Are you a masochist?"

"Valerie likes it," I explain, "and it turns out that Biscuit likes it, too."

At her name, the dog barks a couple of times, and I bend down to rub her ears.

"So, how's it going with this woman of yours?" Dad asks.

"It's going fine," I say. "But you don't get to meet her anytime soon. Don't even ask. I'm afraid you'll scare her off."

"Us?" my mom says, looking at my father with faux innocence. "We would never."

One of my exes broke up with me shortly after meeting my parents, and I've always wondered...but anyway, it doesn't matter. Meeting my family isn't what Valerie needs right now, even if I've already met hers.

"Ben is still traumatized," Mackenzie says.

"Then Ben is a wuss!" Mom shoots back.

Sometimes I wonder how I turned out so normal.

"Anyway," Dad says, "dinner will be ready soon. You want to set the table, Peter?"

Ah, an innocuous task.

I jump at the chance.

When I get home that evening, I text Valerie.

ME: I miss you.

VALERIE: Miss you too. How was dinner with your parents?

ME: Oh, the usual.

I decide not to go into details.

VALERIE: Chloe and I are having boba.

She sends me a photo of her sipping bubble tea through a pink straw. I can't help picturing her mouth wrapped around something else, but I manage to push that aside by thinking about my parents buying lingerie.

Still, I continue to stare at the photo, an ache in my chest as I think of all the things I want for her. Not only do I want her to have the career she loves, but I also want her to be able to move out, either to live with me or by herself.

When I got home from work the other day and Valerie came to the door to greet me, I was filled with longing for that to be my future. Except ideally she would have a Monday-to-Friday job in software development, and she might not be home to meet me at five o'clock.

Instead, maybe I'd be the one making after-work tea for her, rushing to the door to greet her with a kiss.

Yeah, I like that picture. I like thinking about our future, but I fear I'm getting too far ahead of myself, when we haven't exchanged *I love you*s.

I ask her something else instead.

> ME: Can I visit you tomorrow at Ginger
> Scoops when I finish work?

> VALERIE: Sure

I can't help but smile, but it's tinged with sadness.
What if this doesn't work out? How could I bear it?

Chapter 23

Valerie

IT'S NOT VERY WARM out, but Peter and I are sitting on the patio at Ginger Scoops, wearing our fall jackets. He's wearing a toque, too.

Sure, we could have sat inside, but I want a break from being inside Ginger Scoops. It feels a bit claustrophobic after a while. Peter isn't complaining about sitting outdoors, and he looks cute in that gray hat, I'm not going to lie.

He slides an envelope across the table. A pink envelope with my name on the front.

Inside, there's a kirigami pop-up card with two swans.

I almost start crying.

Oh my God, what's wrong with me?

But my boyfriend is so sweet and I can't take it anymore. He's written, *I like when we're together* in the card. Just something simple, but as our gazes collide, I see the truth in his eyes. He has stronger feelings for me, but he's holding back because he knows I'm not ready.

And that makes me want to weep even more. How can I be dating a man who's so kind and thoughtful? How can he care for me so much?

No, he must have a hidden flaw. A major one. A deep, dark secret.

I need to figure out what it is.

"Valerie?" He interlaces his fingers with mine. "Are you okay?"

"Yes. I love the card. It's so sweet. Thank you."

He tilts his head to the side. "If you don't like cards, just tell me. I won't be offended. I can get you something else instead, like a durian bun."

"You're already doing a pretty good job of supplying me with durian."

He pulls my chair toward him and lifts his hand to—

"Peter So! Is that you?"

I turn and see a pretty woman with light brown skin. She's hurrying down the sidewalk toward us—well, toward Peter.

"Deepti." He stands up, and they embrace when she reaches our table. "How are you? It's been five years, maybe more?" He smiles at her. "I heard you were called to the bar."

She takes a seat next to him. "Yes, and now I'm working seventy-hour weeks. Today is unusual—I'm off work at five thirty."

Is Peter going to introduce us? I—

"This is Valerie." He gestures toward me. "My girlfriend. Valerie, this is Deepti. We used to date back in undergrad."

An ex! I'm immediately on high alert. Maybe she's still interested in him. I sneak a peek at my boyfriend—he does look good. I wouldn't blame her.

Then I notice the ring on her finger. It's freaking gigantic and glitters in the sun.

Peter notices, too. "You're engaged!"

"I am."

"Congratulations. When's the big day?"

"Next summer. My mother is driving me crazy with wedding planning."

While they discuss the wedding, I study Deepti. She's wearing a navy trench coat with a gray skirt suit underneath. Her black shoes are perfectly polished. The colorful scarf around her neck prevents her outfit from being too staid. She's the picture of sophistication, whereas I'm...well. Me.

When I try to tune back into the conversation, Deepti is looking at me expectantly.

"Uh, sorry. Did you say something?"

"How long have you two been together?" she asks.

"Oh, not long."

"We met because she spilled durian ice cream all over me," Peter says.

"Durian!" Deepti bursts into laughter. "Remember when—"

"How could I forget?"

They're sharing some kind of private joke about durian, and I feel left out, but Peter isn't showing any interest in Deepti. They're just old friends catching up. It would be foolish to be jealous.

"How's your family?" he asks.

"We're doing well. My sister just finished her degree in biology at Guelph."

Peter shakes his head. "I still think of her as twelve. I can't imagine her with a degree."

"What about you? What are you up to these days?"

"Landscaping. Nothing too exciting, just living life." He smiles. It's the smile of someone who's content with what he has and where he is in life, even if it's nothing exciting.

I wonder what that would be like.

I thought I had everything I wanted, but that's a distant memory now, and as it turned out, I was actually pretty clueless.

Peter isn't clueless, though. He's just an easygoing, happy guy.

He squeezes my leg under the table and winks at me. There's a gorgeous, sophisticated woman sitting next to him, but I can't doubt his devotion.

There has to be something wrong with him.

The thought pops into my head again. I can't shake it.

And I have the perfect source right in front of me.

"Deepti," I say, "can I talk to you for a minute?"

She looks puzzled but follows me into Ginger Scoops. I lead her to a table by the window and glance outside at Peter, who's drinking his coffee. He waves at me before turning to look at the sidewalk, though he must be wondering what the hell is going on.

"What's up?" Deepti asks.

I get right to the point. "Tell me the truth. What's wrong with Peter?"

She furrows her brow. "Nothing's wrong with him."

"Why'd you break up?"

"I didn't love him enough. He's a great guy, but there wasn't enough spark, you know? You have no reason to be jealous."

"I know, I know." I shake my head. "There *is* enough spark between us, it's just... I can't shake the feeling that this is too good to be true."

My God, I'm really doing this. I hardly know Deepti, yet I'm bombarding her with my insecurities.

"If you had to pick," I say, "what's Peter's greatest flaw?"

"Alright. Let me tell you..."

I lean forward. Okay, this is it.

"He doesn't have much ambition," she says.

"What?"

"It used to bother me that I had all these plans for the future, and he was more of a go-with-the-flow kind of guy. Not that he's lazy. He's not afraid of a little work. But I had big dreams, and he didn't. Unless he's changed, but I don't think he has."

"Oh."

It's not the big reveal I was hoping for.

In fact, I realize this is one of the things I *like* about Peter. He doesn't work so hard that he forgets to enjoy himself, forgets to stop and smell the roses. He has time for me, his friends, his family.

Whereas I could be pretty intense back at my old job and when I was in university.

And Stephen was ambitious, and he was using me to get what he wanted in life. I'd help him with his apps and give him advice for his nine-to-five job, too. I did a lot of things for him, yet he spoke as though these apps were all his own creation. Never acknowledged how much was my doing. A story that's repeated itself over and over in history—a woman spends lots of time helping a man with his work, and he gets all the credit.

So it's actually nice to be with someone who I know won't use me in his career. Who won't get so wrapped up in his job that he'll forget about my existence for a week or more.

Peter might not be the ideal partner for someone like Deepti, but he is for me.

"Valerie?" she says. "Are you okay?"

"I'm sorry," I whisper. "You only just met me, and I know I'm acting like a weirdo. But I was in a terrible relationship before, and that's my only experience with relationships. Peter is so good to me, but I can't help thinking that I must be missing something obvious, like last time. Or he's keeping secrets from me or...I don't know."

"Peter and I were together for over a year," Deepti says. "Trust me, what you see is what you get. He's a good guy."

I blow out a breath. I'm a bit relieved, but I still can't feel completely at ease.

"He was my first boyfriend," she continues, "and I remember him fondly. I'm lucky to have had a good first relationship, and every man I dated afterward, I compared to Peter. When they didn't treat me as well as he had, I knew I could do better, and those guys never lasted long. For a while, I worried that I'd let go of the best guy who'd ever love me, but then I met Kris, and we're a better fit than Peter and I ever were. I can imagine it's hard for you, but you can trust him."

Deepti has been so nice to tell me as much as she has. I turn toward the counter. "Chloe?"

"Yep?"

"Get something for Deepti, whatever she wants."

"No, no," Deepti says. "It's not necessary."

"I work here," I say. "I can do whatever I want. Right, Chloe?"

"Of course."

"The durian ice cream is my favorite, but I know it's not everyone's thing. We have a mango-black sesame swirl for Halloween. The Vietnamese coffee and ginger are probably our most popular flavors."

"Well," Deepti says, "I wouldn't say no to Vietnamese coffee ice cream. Just a small cone."

"No problem." Chloe starts scooping out the ice cream as Deepti and I stand up.

"What's the story with you and Peter and durian?" I ask Deepti.

"Oh." There's a faint blush on her cheeks. "Alright, I'll tell you."

"If it's embarrassing, you don't have to."

"No, it's okay. It's a good story. The first time Peter and I planned to have sex, he had a romantic night planned. After a nice dinner—well, what qualifies as nice when you're eighteen—we were making out in his dorm room, and there was a strange smell. Like natural gas. It was awful, and it started to turn me off. Not exactly the height of romance, you know? Then the fire alarm went off, and we were outside for an hour in the middle of January, until the firemen discovered it wasn't a gas leak, but a durian."

"Wow. That's quite the story."

"It is." Chloe hands Deepti her ice cream cone.

"Thank you for, uh, reassuring me," I say.

"No problem," Deepti says kindly. "I get it. Women have to look out for each other."

I wouldn't have blamed her if she hadn't reacted well to me dragging her into the ice cream shop and asking her questions, but she's been so cool about this.

She waves at me as she steps out the door.

Chloe turns to me. "Did you get the information you wanted? She's Peter's ex, I gather."

"Yeah. She told me that he's a good person."

"But..."

"Why do you think there's a 'but'?"

"You don't look like someone who just got positive news."

"It still seems too good to be true," I whisper.

"Oh, Valerie."

I go outside to meet Peter, and he smiles at me, but it doesn't meet his eyes.

I feel guilty for doubting him, but I can't help it.

Chapter 24

Peter

I don't ask Valerie what she said to Deepti. I already have a pretty good idea.

My girlfriend has doubts about my character. She saw an opportunity to question someone whom she figured would give her an honest answer, and she took it.

Judging by Valerie's expression, Deepti didn't say anything bad about me. I wouldn't have expected her to.

I hate that Valerie doesn't seem to trust me as much as I thought she did. I want to snap at her, ask her what I did to deserve this when I think I've been the perfect boyfriend.

But I know it's not about me.

After everything that happened last year, she can't help her suspicions, and it breaks my heart to think about what she's been through.

I have to give her more time, but what if this doesn't work out, just like all my other relationships? Valerie is special, and I know she's the right woman for me...and I would hope that means we can make this work. That it will be different from what I've had in the past.

But what if it isn't? What if this, too, comes to an end?

What if she decides it isn't worth it? What if she can never completely trust me?

I've had many break-ups. I know how much they can suck...and I think this would be the worst one yet.

For now, I'll try to be patient and hope that she comes around. Hope that soon I can say "I love you," and know she's prepared to hear it. Usually, I'm good at being patient, but it's hard when I want something so much.

We walk around the city for an hour, holding hands, occasionally making conversation.

I don't want this to be temporary. I want it to be my future.

Chapter 25

Valerie

It's Friday night, and once again, I'm waiting for my mother to come home from playing mahjong with her friends.

But this time, I don't feel pathetic for getting home before my mother. I've been more social lately, hanging out with Peter on a regular basis. In fact, I was out until nearly one tonight.

And now it's two.

Hmm. If Mom keeps this up, she might get another parking ticket.

I'm trying to read as I drink a cup of tea, but my gaze keep straying to the kirigami swan card that I'm using as a bookmark. I read over the message. *I like when we're together.*

After I finished work, Peter and I went out for a late dinner at the bar with the decadent chocolate cake—which we had again, of course—and danced to the live band. And kissed in Graffiti Alley. I like that we have "our" places now.

Still, doubts continue to crowd my head.

There has to be something wrong with him.

No, you're just being paranoid!

All men are assholes.

Not all men!

Ugh, the voices in my head are so annoying.

The front door opens.

"Valerie!" my mother shouts.

I head to the front hall. "Stop screaming. You'll wake Dad and Sabrina."

"I don't care!"

"Are you drunk? Was someone slipping brandy into the tea?"

"Wah, silly girl! I do not drink and drive. No, it's Peter! You won't believe what Daphne told me." Mom tugs off her shoes and puts on her slippers before heading to the kitchen. "He has been lying to you all along."

I feel a bizarre kind of relief. I was right to be suspicious.

Sabrina hurries downstairs in her pajamas. "What's wrong?"

"Your sister's boyfriend!" Mom says. "I should have known."

"Peter?"

"Yes, Peter," I snap. "The guy you were ogling at Thanksgiving."

At least Sabrina has the decency to look embarrassed.

Not that it matters. Because Peter has been lying to me.

"What is it, Mom?" I ask.

Unfortunately, she insists on putting on the kettle and taking out some cookies before she'll say anything.

By the time she sits down at the table with me and Sabrina, I'm practically shaking. I can't stand this anymore. I need to know what my boyfriend did.

"You know Daphne's niece, Justine?" Mom says.

"Yes," I say impatiently.

"She went to med school and graduated in the same year as Peter claimed he did. But Justine is certain there was no Peter in her year, and she looked up 'Peter So' on Facebook and found your handsome Peter. He is not a pediatrician. He's in landscaping!"

Oh.

Well, that was rather anticlimactic.

"I know," I sigh.

"*You know?*"

"Yeah." I might as well tell the truth now. It has to happen at some point. "I told Peter to pretend he was a doctor so you'd like him. In fact, the night you got a parking ticket—"

"That law is such garbage!"

"—was the first time I mentioned having a boyfriend, if you remember. Auntie Minnie didn't think I was good enough for Kent Lo, and I wanted to show you that I could get a guy you respected. So I made up a pediatrician named Peter, and when I met a guy named Peter at Ginger Scoops, I thought I'd take the lie a little further and ask him to be my fake boyfriend."

God, this makes me sound like a loon.

"Wait a minute," Mom says. "Peter is not actually your boyfriend?"

"He is now."

"I am getting a headache."

"Maybe you shouldn't stay out until two in the morning playing mahjong."

"Maybe my daughters shouldn't make my life so difficult."

"Hey," Sabrina says. "What did I do? This is all Valerie."

"You are majoring in English and film studies!"

"Right, right, I forgot that's a sin."

"Peter majored in English, too," I say.

"I liked him better when he was a doctor." Mom sniffs.

"He was never a doctor."

"But I didn't know that! You are serious, Valerie? You knew the truth all along and were lying to your poor, beleaguered mother?"

"You are not poor and beleaguered. And yes, I knew the truth all along. It was my idea, like I said."

The water boils, and my mother gets up to make a cup of tea. Sabrina and I watch in horrified fascination as she grabs a small bottle of brandy from behind the cornstarch and pours a generous amount into her cup.

"I think that will hide the flavor of the tea," I say.

"I don't care! Wah, I can't believe this. I was so proud of my daughter for landing a handsome pediatrician, and it was all a lie."

"Does it really matter?" I ask. "Who cares if he's a doctor? He treats me well. Why are you so concerned about appearances?"

She clucks her tongue. "You think making people's gardens pretty is just as good as saving lives?"

"Enough!" I howl. "Not everyone can be a doctor—or even a doctor of rocks."

"What's going on down here?"

It's my father, standing in the doorway to the kitchen.

"Peter isn't a doctor!" Mom shouts.

"I know," Dad says.

"*What*?"

"I looked him up online after he came over for Thanksgiving."

"Why didn't you tell me?"

"Because I wanted to avoid this?" He gestures feebly.

"Did you know that Valerie knew the truth?"

"No..."

"You thought your own daughter might be dating a liar, and you didn't say anything? Aiyah! What is wrong with you? I came home and immediately told Valerie!"

"And woke me up!"

"Ah, your precious sleep. It's always about your precious sleep..."

Sabrina and I look at each other and silently agree to get out from the middle of the argument. We tiptoe upstairs, although why the hell we're tiptoeing, I have no idea. It's two thirty in the morning, but everyone's awake.

At the top of the stairs, Sabrina gives me a hug. I stand there for a moment in surprise before hugging her back—my family isn't the touchy-feely sort.

"I can't believe it," she says. "You had a fake boyfriend! That's so cool."

I'm flummoxed that my sister considers this "cool" rather than "pathetic," but I'll take it.

"You always seemed, well...rather boring," she continues.

"You could have stopped talking after you called me cool."

She grins. "It's just like *To All the Boys I've Loved Before!* Remember we watched that together? You secretly enjoyed it, even though you pretended otherwise. Why do you pretend not to like romance and things that are considered feminine? Was it a way of trying to fit in in your male-dominated profession?" Before I can answer, she says, "Ooh, is that why you named your fake boyfriend 'Peter'? After the guy in the movie?"

"It is," I admit.

"I'm glad you found someone. Peter is much better than Stephen. Where did he study English?"

"Queen's. That part of the story wasn't a lie, just his major."

She nods. "That gives us something in common to talk about next time."

"Don't you dare show any interest in him. He's taken."

"I mean, talk about in a friendly, brother-sister kind of way."

I raise my eyebrows. "Brother-sister kind of way?"

"I assume you're going to marry him one day."

I open my mouth, but no words come out.

"Me. Marry. Him?" I finally splutter.

"Well, you should. Since you make each other happy and I doubt you can do any better."

"Sabrina—"

"That wasn't an insult. I'm just saying he's great—for *you*."

"Yeah," I say quietly. "He is."

Twenty minutes later, once my parents have turned down the volume on their argument, I snuggle up under my covers, waiting for sleep to overtake me.

But I keep thinking of Peter.

I'm paranoid after what happened with Stephen, but unlike when I was in university, I've been on the look-out for warning signs from the very beginning. Thinking back, there were so many issues with my ex, but I either didn't see them or pretended they were no big deal. I was naïve and willing to overlook a lot for the first guy who'd wanted a real relationship with me.

Peter is different, though, and even if I'm a bit of a pain in the ass, he cares for me. He doesn't show it with excessive roses or chocolates, or fancy dinners; everything he does is more low-key, but it's just for *me*.

Taking me to the durian shop. Letting me have a whole day alone in his apartment. Giving me cards that are sweet, but not painfully mushy.

I'm in a happy, healthy relationship with a decent guy.

And it's still hard to wrap my mind around that.

I'm scooping out some matcha cheesecake ice cream for a young woman when I feel a prickle on the back of my neck.

Sometimes this happens when Peter is near. I have a strange feeling of awareness, even before I see or hear him.

But this time, it's different. Unpleasant.

I'm immediately on edge.

I continue scooping the ice cream, giving the woman more than a single scoop, afraid to glance up. Perhaps it's one of those idiotic men who tell me to smile more or compliment my "almond-shaped" eyes.

This weird sixth sense doesn't make sense to my logical brain, but I trust it.

And when I look up, after giving change to the customer, Stephen Shum is standing in front of me.

I wasn't expecting anything good, but this is a surprise.

"Get out," someone says.

It's not me—I still haven't found my voice.

It's Chloe.

"Hey, hey." Stephen holds up his hands. "I'm not here to make a scene. I just want to talk to Valerie for a few minutes."

"Valerie has nothing to say to you, you asshole. Get the *fuck* out of my shop."

This is out of character for Chloe. It's not like she never swears—she totally does—but she's a sweet person who never swears *at* someone quite like this.

Stephen definitely merits swearing, though.

"I came to apologize," he says.

"She's moved on. She doesn't need your goddamn apology."

Chloe's face is red with rage and she's holding her fist, as though restraining herself from reaching across the counter and punching him.

I appreciate having a friend who feels so much indignation on my behalf.

However...

Maybe I do need to talk to Stephen for closure.

Although closure is one of those wishy-washy things that I'm not sure I entirely believe in, I can't help being curious about what he wants to say to me. And while I've started dating again, my past is still affecting me, and I haven't tried to change where I am career-wise.

Yes, it will be hard without any references, with the gap in my resume, but I need to give it a try. Peter and my brother are right: that's what I want to do with my life. Lately, I've been missing it more and more.

But I haven't been able to consider it without freaking the fuck out.

What happened with Stephen was tied to my career, too. Maybe talking to him will help, though more than anything, I want to tell him off.

I wouldn't have been strong enough to handle this before, but I am now.

"Okay." I blow out a breath. "We can meet at the coffee shop down the street. Ten minutes, nothing more."

"You don't have to do it," Chloe whispers.

"It's okay," I tell her. "I've got this."

A couple of minutes later, Stephen and I are sitting in the coffee shop.

"You don't have long," I say. "As soon as I finish this coffee, I'm out of here."

"I always liked that about you. You're direct."

"Get to the fucking point."

There's a ghost of a smile on his lips. "I'm sorry I cheated on you and blamed you for, uh, not meeting my sexual needs. I'm now pretty sure that I wasn't meeting yours."

"Wow." I fold my arms over my chest. "That's a surprising amount of insight, coming from you."

"Give me another chance." He leans forward. "You're the only woman I've ever loved."

"Such a cliché."

"We were together for a long time. We lived together. And now you're brushing me off?"

"Stephen, it was a year ago. I've moved on. I have a boyfriend—"

"Really?"

"Why are you surprised? If you want me back, you must think I'm desirable."

"I do." He shifts his hand toward me on the table, and I slap it away. "You're not going to make this easy for me, are you?"

"Why would I make anything easy for you after what you did to me? But there's no chance in hell of us getting back together. You need to get that weird fantasy out of your head."

His lips thin. He's not used to being told he can't have what he wants; he's a spoiled only son.

"At least come work for me," he says.

"Work for you?"

"I thought you'd heard. I started my own company."

"Mm. Fascinating."

"Can you cut the sarcasm?"

"Nope."

He rolls his eyes. "You're better than working at an ice cream shop. You have a degree."

"Stop it. There's nothing wrong with my job."

"Sorry. I just mean that it's not making use of your skills. You were passionate about what you did before."

"You heard the details of what happened?"

"Yes, which is why I want to offer you a job."

"So kind of you."

"Valerie."

"You used me," I say, my voice trembling. "You never acknowledged it because it would have been too much for your precious ego to bear, but I'm better at certain things than you.

You asked for my advice on a regular basis, and I gave it to you freely. You never thanked me. You never told me I was smart. It wasn't just a quick question here and there. It was a lot, Stephen, and not just that. There was so much broken in our relationship, not just the sex"—I dart my eyes around the shop, a little embarrassed to be having this conversation—"but unfortunately, I didn't know any better then. But I do now, and I want nothing to do with you." I pause. "You know what's fucked up? When my boss hit on me, I told Chloe, not you, because I worried you'd say something about me leading him on. I didn't trust you, even before you cheated on me."

I'm full of fury now. At Stephen. At myself for staying in that relationship so long.

"I don't think you remember—" he begins.

"Guess what?" I drain the rest of my coffee and slap the mug on the table. It makes a satisfying thud. "I remember just perfectly, and I know you're a piece of shit. I'm glad you've done some learning and are a slightly—slightly, mind you—smaller piece of shit now, but I don't give a fuck. I have someone else, and I'm happy, goddammit, I'm happy. And if I was single, I'd still be happier than I was with you. I'm happier working at an ice cream shop than I would be working for you." I shudder. "God, I can't imagine the horror."

"Stop being so dramatic. I can give you the chance you deserve."

"There are other people who would give me a chance, too."

"Who?"

I glower at him. "I'm leaving. I would say it was nice to see you, but it definitely wasn't."

I stalk toward the door, and another woman in the coffee shop gives me a smile and a thumbs-up.

When I saw Stephen, I didn't feel even the slightest bit of affection, didn't recall any nice memories. There is nothing in my heart for him. Nothing.

Good.

He doesn't deserve it.

I wasn't planning to visit Peter after work, but I need to see him. I need to feel his arms around me.

"Stephen came by today," I say as soon as I step inside his apartment.

Peter stiffens. "What happened?"

"He wants me back. Apparently, he's started his own company and he wants me to work for him, too."

"What did you do?"

"I told him off."

"Good."

"It was nice to say all that shit to his face, but now I'm…"

Now that I'm with Peter, the lingering adrenaline that was pumping through my veins disappears. I feel drained.

He leads me to his couch and pulls me into his lap, and he just holds me. He tightens his arms around me and nuzzles my neck, and I feel safe. Cherished.

When his lips press against mine, I open for him, and we share a slow kiss, as if we're moving through honey.

I love you.

The words slam into my brain like a ton of bricks, leaving me off-balance.

It's true, though. It's utterly true. I love Peter, and I love who I am when we're together.

I'm prickly, I'm not exactly sweet-tempered, but all of that is okay with him. He's willing to be there no matter what. He likes me for who I am, but at the same time, he makes me a stronger person.

I want to say it out loud, but I can't.

The words are stuck in my throat.

I've only exchanged those words with one man before, the man I saw earlier today, and that relationship didn't end well.

It's scary to be in love. It's scary to have this level of intimacy with someone.

But Peter is nothing like Stephen. I was freaking out before, convinced there had to be something wrong with Peter, convinced that such a kind, amazing man couldn't actually be with me.

However, my doubts have been erased, more or less.

I thought Deepti would give me dirt on Peter. When my mother said Peter had been lying to me, I thought surely, it was something bad.

But, no. It isn't too good to be true. This is really happening.

It's so perfect, I still have trouble believing it, and I'm too frightened to say "I love you," even though I know he'll say it back.

After seeing Stephen, I'm vulnerable, scraped raw. I'm pissed at myself for not being able to declare my love, but I can't help it.

I love Peter, and although our relationship has been real for a while, it's now terrifyingly real in a way it wasn't before, and I have the urge to bolt.

"What's up?" Peter turns me so we're facing each other.

"I'm scared." This is the adult thing to do, to talk about how I feel, even if I can't say everything.

"What are you afraid of?"

I gesture between us. "Being close to someone. I hate myself for feeling like this—"

"You don't—"

"—because I know you won't treat me like Stephen did, but since I suck at intimacy, that's my only other experience. I tell myself that logically, I shouldn't feel this way, but I still do. How have you had so many relationships? I can't imagine opening myself up that many times."

He runs a hand through my hair. Soothing. "There's nothing wrong with you."

I release a shuddering breath.

There's nothing wrong with me.

He's right, but I felt otherwise for so long.

"I thought this was too good to be true, but it isn't," I say. "Though I still can't help worrying, but I know I have to take a risk to have something wonderful and..." I shake my head. "Why is this all so difficult?"

Why can't I tell you how I really feel?

"Valerie." He puts his hands on my cheeks and looks me in the eyes. "What do you need? Tell me what you need, and I'll give it to you."

I blow out a breath. I won't give in to my urge to run away forever. But...

"I need some space. A break."

"A break," he repeats.

"This has all happened so fast, from being in a fake relationship, to being in a real one, to..." *To realizing I love you.* "I know I shouldn't need this, when you're so kind and understanding, but I do. I will come back to you, I promise. I just need some space for a few days."

He nods and looks down. "Okay."

It makes me want to cry, the way he's willing to give this to me so easily, just because I asked, even though I'm sure it's not what he wants. Because Peter, unlike me, doesn't seem to be dealing with any crazy fears or insecurities. He's calm and confident and everything I wish I could be but am not. He loves me, I have no doubt; I know it sounds corny, but I can feel it in the way he touches me, in his every word. He's been holding back, though, because he knows I can't handle hearing those words yet.

How is he so perfect? How is he mine?

But he is. I know this.

He wraps me tightly in his arms and kisses my hair.

"Goodbye for now," he says.

Chapter 26

Peter

"Hey, girl!" I say. "We've been at the dog park for half an hour. Time to go home."

Biscuit glances at me, thoroughly unimpressed, and goes back to chewing her stick.

Even the dog doesn't love me.

Okay, I have to stop being so melodramatic. Valerie just needs some space, so I'm giving her space. She says she'll come back to me, and I'm trying to believe her.

But this feels as bad as a break-up, and I should know. I've had a lot of break-ups. Thirteen, to be exact.

I can't help thinking about the what-ifs. Usually, I'm not much of a worrier, and I can push these thoughts to the side.

Today is different, though.

What if she changes her mind? What if that was goodbye forever?

I didn't tell her about my fears. I didn't think she needed to deal with those.

The fact is, however, that the two "breaks" I've had in relationships ultimately led to the end. I just need to do my best to have faith that it won't happen again.

Biscuit finally trots over and deposits her stick at my feet. I put on her leash and we head back to my parents' house, where we snuggle on the couch, a pitiful pair. Me and the dog, watching the hockey game together.

A few minutes later, my dad comes in.

"Peter! You didn't tell us you were coming over today."

"I didn't come here to see you. I came to see Biscuit."

"Gee, thanks. Way to make your old man feel wanted."

Things are simpler with Biscuit. She doesn't ask for explanations. She just happily accepts snuggles and ignores me at the dog park.

"Where's Mom?" I ask.

"Oh, she's at an art class."

When Dad provides no further details, I assume that means my mother is posing nude for life sketching.

I try not to think about it.

"Did you and Valerie break up?" Dad asks. "Is that why you're down in the dumps?"

"We didn't break up. We're taking a break."

He snorts. "When does that ever work out?"

I don't say anything.

I miss Valerie so much. I'm not used to going a whole day without texting her. I'm not used to going a few days without meeting her at Ginger Scoops.

This isn't the end, right?

I go back to my apartment that Saturday evening, after having dinner with my parents. I turn on my TV and pull up Netflix, but I can't manufacture an interest in anything, so I turn off the TV and throw the remote to the other side of the couch.

Goddammit.

I try to get up, but I can't muster the enthusiasm.

Finally, I convince myself to go to the fridge for a beer. I told Valerie that I like IPAs, and she went to a brewery in Etobicoke that had just released a new batch of what is supposed to be an excellent IPA, which you can only get at the brewery. I grab one from the top shelf and manage to injure myself while opening the bottle.

God*dammit*.

I take the beer back to the couch and put on a movie I've seen a zillion times before, something I don't have to pay much attention to, because my brain is still focused on Valerie.

I remember all the things we did together.

The kissing. The dancing. The sex.

The Japanese cheesecake, Korean-Polish fusion, Thai rolled ice cream, flourless chocolate cake, pupusas... Fuck, will I even be able to go out for food in Toronto without her haunting me?

I remember coming home from work and finding her in the bath, drinking wine. Another time, she scurried to the door and gave me a kiss.

I remember her telling me about her ex and her job.

I know it's hard for Valerie to talk about those things. I know it's been hard for her to open up to me, to go to bed with me.

Yet she's faced her fears. She's stronger than she believes.

I admire the hell out of her.

And one day soon, she'll find her way back to her career, and I know she will kick ass.

I hope she'll let me be by her side.

I slap my bottle of beer on the table and turn off the TV. I can't stand to sit here any longer. My inclination is to go to Ginger Scoops, but I need to give her the space she asked for. I need to be patient.

Instead, I go to the Thai rolled ice cream place and order the same thing that Valerie and I shared. Chocolate-strawberry.

Except this time, I eat it all by myself, and I don't bother taking any Instagram pictures.

Afterward, I head to the bar where we went dancing and have another beer. Then I go to Graffiti Alley, where I walk past two couples making out and a bunch of teenagers smoking pot.

I've never acted like this after a break-up. Never moped about the city, reliving our dates.

I wasn't wrong; I really never have felt this way before.

I can't regret my previous relationships, and they were what I wanted at the time. But now, I'm committed to building a future with Valerie. I will do whatever it takes.

I'd buy a durian, smash it open with an ax, and eat the whole goddamn thing if that would convince her of my commitment. I'd even eat a pint of durian ice cream every week for the rest of my life if it meant I get to be with her.

Of course, that wouldn't be preferable, but I'd do it. Not that Valerie would expect me to suffer like that for her.

I have to trust her the way I want her to trust me, and when she comes back to me—I tell myself it's "when," not "if"—I'll be everything she deserves.

Chapter 27

Valerie

Sunday night, I'm hanging out at Sarah's apartment with my friends. There's khao soi, pad Thai, beef massaman curry, and rice on the table before us, and we're already on our second bottle of wine. I'm full, but that doesn't stop me from taking seconds of the massaman curry.

It's like I keep eating to fill up the emptiness inside me that comes from missing Peter, but there's no food that could make up for Peter, of course.

Not even every dessert from Doctor Durian.

I was convinced I needed time apart, but it hasn't helped me feel ready to say "I love you." And I still feel like this is something I need to sort out by myself before I can go back to him. I need to let go of some of my fears about relationships.

I tell myself over and over that Peter is nothing like Stephen and he would never do anything to hurt me. I know that in my bones.

But knowing my fears are irrational doesn't stop me from feeling that way.

I've come so far with Peter. When I invented a relationship to please my mother, I never could have imagined being in this position a couple of months later.

Once my friends and I finish all the Thai food—I must say, I'm impressed we managed it—we move on to dessert: coconut pie with green tea ice cream, plus durian ice cream for me. Nobody else here appreciates durian as much as I do.

I look around the table at my friends, and tears prick at the back of my eyes.

There's Chloe, who's been friends with me since the beginning of high school. Somehow, she's managed to put up with me for more than a decade. Now she has Drew and her ice cream shop—and I'm glad I got to be a part of her dream. She's had some struggles with losing her mother and finding her place in the world, but she's doing well now, and I'm so happy for her.

Then Sarah, whom I haven't known as long, but I see her regularly since she owns the pie shop across the street. We first met when she looked in the window while Chloe and I were painting the back wall of Ginger Scoops. And soon after, Sarah started dating Josh.

She doesn't know what happened before Ginger Scoops. Well, she knows I was a software developer, and I may have told her that men are assholes on numerous occasions, but she doesn't know the details.

I don't want everyone to know, but suddenly, I want to tell Sarah.

It will be easier this time, now that I've done it with Peter.

I finish my coconut pie and durian ice cream, then take a large sip of wine. "I have to tell you something," I say to Sarah. "About what happened before we met."

And so I tell her the story that I told Peter, in slightly less detail. About Stephen, my old job, and my old boss. My week from hell. She doesn't speak much, just mutters "those assholes" a couple of times and squeezes my hand.

By the end, I feel a sense of relief, but I'm also angry.

Maybe that anger will never completely go away, but unlike a year ago, I feel like I could have a future that *I* want. I'm no longer just scrambling to get through each day, putting one foot in front of the other.

Plus, the best revenge is living well, isn't it?

I hate asking for favors, but maybe I should think of it as using connections instead. "Sarah, do you think Josh—"

"Yes."

"You didn't even hear the question!"

"I know what you're going to say." She tops up my wine. "Yes, I'll talk to Josh and find a time for you to go to his office and speak to him. I think they're hiring."

"It doesn't have to be him. I'm sure he's busy. It could be someone else in the company. I don't need special treatment; I just need someone to actually consider me for a job. Or if Hazelnut Tech isn't hiring, maybe he has other ideas for where I could apply."

Sarah places her hand on top of mine. "You'll talk to him and see what happens, okay? One step at a time. And I believe everything you told me, you know that, right?"

"Thank you," I whisper, then turn to Chloe. "I hope to quit my job at Ginger Scoops soon. You'll have to find someone else—"

"Don't worry about it. I never expected you to stay more than six months, and it's not busy now that it's November. It's fine. I want this for you, Valerie."

I nod.

And then I burst into tears.

I didn't cry a year ago. I feared that if I started, I would never stop. I moved on to my new normal of living with my parents and sister and helping Chloe start her ice cream shop. I didn't let myself hope for much.

Now, I can cry, and I don't feel helpless. I'm not much of a crier, but it's nice to let it out.

"I love you two," I say, putting my arms around Chloe and Sarah. "Even though you insist on filling my life with rainbows, unicorns, and pink walls..."

"I know," Chloe says, squeezing my shoulder. "I know."

"I think I'm drunk." I take another sip of wine. "But I meant everything I said, and I will remember it in the morning."

"Do you want to stay here?" Sarah asks. "I doubt you want to go back to Scarborough now. Or you could go to Peter's."

"Peter and I are taking a break."

"*What*? I thought it was going well. What did he do?"

"Nothing. He's wonderful." And then I admit something out loud for the first time. Not to Peter, but maybe it's a start. "I love him."

Chloe smiles at me. "I thought you did."

"I never expected to fall in love again, and I'm too scared to tell him."

My friends nod in understanding. None of them have my past, but Chloe had struggled with close relationships for many years before finding Drew, and Sarah had never had a real relationship until this past year. And I've seen how despite these things, they've managed to make love work with the right person.

I don't feel like talking about it anymore, but I draw strength from being with people who care about me and from what they've managed to do.

Wow, I sure am sappy tonight. All the emotion I usually don't let myself feel is leaking out. I wipe my eyes and smile.

"I'll figure it out, don't worry," I say, and I truly believe that. "Now, is there any more durian ice cream in the freezer?"

·♥·♥·♥·♥·♥·

When Mom comes home from mahjong on Monday, it's only midnight. I'm sitting at the kitchen table with my laptop and a cup of tea.

"Daphne was cheating, I swear," Mom grumbles. "No way she got that lucky." She hangs up her keys. "What are you working on?"

"My resume."

"Ah, you're going back to a proper job. Good."

I roll my eyes. "I already have a proper job. It's just not what I want to do with my life."

"I know. That's what I meant."

"My friend's boyfriend has a mobile app and custom software company. I'm going to talk to him tomorrow."

"Good, good."

I close my laptop. "Mom, do you believe me?"

"What do you mean? I believe you about what?"

"About what my boss did."

"Of course I believe you. You think I don't know this stuff happens? You think it didn't happen to me?"

That never occurred to me, no, even though it's a common experience.

"You didn't approve of me quitting my job right away," I say.

"It's not what I would have done, but maybe that is wrong. How can I expect my daughter to put up with that kind of boss?"

"It wasn't that bad, not compared to what some women have to deal with." That's something I've thought several times in the past year: it could have been worse.

"It was still inappropriate. Plus, who knows what he would have done next. No, I thought about it more, and I'm glad you quit. You were lucky to have a choice. You would not be homeless without that job because you could always live with us."

Yes, in some ways, I'm quite lucky. I could speak up without fearing that I wouldn't have a roof over my head or food on the table. Not every woman is in such a position.

It's on the tip of my tongue to ask my mom more questions, ones about her life before she met my father and came to Canada.

But I know she won't tell me.

My mother loves secrets.

She doesn't love *me* keeping secrets—she wants to pry and know every detail of my life—but she has her own.

"I was angry at the situation, not at you," she says. "Worried you would struggle to find a new job and have the career you wanted. And that's what happened. Your colleague, he gave you a bad reference, yes?"

I nod.

"Lack of security...it scares me. The—what do you call it? Patriarchy. It can destroy women's careers. I know you think I just care about appearances, but I saw how proud you were of the work you did. Though you didn't even want to take a computer science course at first, do you remember that?"

I do. I thought I'd be bad at it. I don't know why; I was generally a good student, and I'd already taught myself some HTML for LiveJournal. Fortunately, my dad convinced me to take it in grade ten, and I discovered I had an aptitude for it.

"I saw how you loved figuring things out," Mom says. "I want that career for you because it's what you want for yourself, even if you sometimes pretend you can live without it. And yes, I like to brag, too, I will not lie."

"What about Peter? Are you still disappointed he's not a doctor?"

I don't tell her that we're on a break. I think it would just confuse her.

"I was mainly upset that he was lying to you!"

"But I told you, he wasn't lying to me. It was all my idea."

"Silly girl, inventing boyfriends."

"I did it because I didn't want to be a disappointment to you."

"You are not a disappointment! Well, sometimes, but not most of the time." She pauses. "I have so much respect for doctors. Plus, good job, good money. So I thought it would be nice if one of you was a doctor, or married a doctor. And Peter reminded me of one of the doctors in the NICU when you were little, too little." Her normally strong voice wavers. "I came to Canada to start a new life. I got pregnant, all was good, then..." She shakes her head. "Aiyah, I will make a scene."

"Mom, it's just me here, no one else."

She hesitates. "You were sick, and I thought maybe I was being punished for..." She doesn't finish that thought, and I'm not surprised. She said something similar once before but refused to tell me what she meant. "But the doctors and nurses were good. Eventually, I brought you home, you turned out okay."

"Thanks, Mom."

"You took so long to learn to talk. I was worried, but then you were so smart, especially with numbers." She sighs. "Anyway, Peter is fine, if he treats you better than Stephen. Stephen seemed like a good boy, but he did terrible things to you."

"Peter is very different from Stephen."

"So, I approve. I think you will make cute babies."

"Mom!"

She laughs. "It's okay, you can worry about that later. I'm going to bed now."

She goes upstairs, and so do I, after putting the finishing touches on my resume.

The informal interview with Josh goes well. We talk about the work I used to do, and at the end, he offers me a job in the custom software division. He tells me about some of the projects they have right now, and it all sounds good to me. I just want to do something, anything. Get my foot in the door.

Afterward, I stand at the corner of Yonge and Queen, the Eaton Centre across the road, and debate where to go. I'm wearing my trench coat, which isn't quite warm enough in the November weather, and a "business casual" outfit. I didn't want to dress up too much for the interview, knowing Josh always dresses casually; I wanted to look like I would fit in.

He won't regret hiring me. I have the skills to do this job, and I can be great at it, I know.

I stand there at the corner, with the cool November wind in my hair, and I smile.

But then I'm overcome with agony, an aching emptiness inside me. I miss Peter so much. I wish he were here to share this moment with me.

"I love you," I whisper into the wind, unable to keep the words inside.

The time apart has made it clearer than ever that I love him, and I've started to feel at peace with my overwhelming feelings. I've had time to accept them, and after talking to Sarah and Chloe and my mother, I'm less afraid and can see a way forward. I no longer feel like running away.

But I think part of the problem was that I felt like I had to be perfect before I could declare my love for Peter. I had to have the job lined up first, and I wanted to take that step by myself, although it's not like he could have done the interview for me anyway.

Even if it's been a while since we spoke, part of the reason I was able to do this was because of him. He believes in me, and he helped me to really start living again, rather than just going through the motions. My friends helped, too.

I needed those months of working for Chloe. I don't regret them. After the disappointment from those interviews, I was in a rough place, and as I told her, I'm glad I got to be part of her dream.

Now, however, it's time to move on, and I'm lucky I have this opportunity.

Sadly, there's no guarantee I'll never be harassed like that again at work, but I'm not going to let those assholes keep me from what I want to do. And there are people who will support me, no matter what.

Alright. I'm going to have a chicken pot pie at Happy as Pie for lunch, and then I'm going to Peter's apartment—I still have his key—to prepare for when he comes home from work. I have a few ideas.

Although there's no way to be sure it'll last forever, I have a really good feeling about us. Plus, it's worth the risk for something this great.

Peter might not have said everything he feels out loud, but I trust in his feelings for me.

And now, I'm ready to talk.

Chapter 28

Peter

"Here you go." The concierge hands me a small box, which was delivered while I was at work.

"Thank you."

I know exactly what this is.

It's the U-shaped vibrator I ordered for Valerie.

I haven't seen her since last week. I've been giving her the space she requested and hoping, every day when I come home from work, that she'll be in my apartment—either in the bathtub with a glass of wine or...

Hell, I don't care, as long as she's there.

I take the elevator up to my floor, snickering as I look at the box.

God, I miss her.

I put my key in the lock and turn it, and when I step inside, something seems different. Smells different.

I glance toward the kitchen, and my mouth falls open. There's food on every inch of the table and covering half the counter. That must mean...

"Hey." Valerie steps out from my bedroom. "You're home early."

I take off my boots and walk toward her. "You're here."

"I'm here."

We're quiet for a moment.

Valerie is wearing a light blue blouse and gray pants. She's a little more dressed up than usual, and she's utterly lovely of course.

"I got a job," she says. "I start in two weeks."

"That's amazing!"

"It's with Josh's company. I had an interview this morning, and he was impressed with what I'd done before. It'll take a little while to get back into it, but..." She grins. "I'm thrilled."

I lift her off the ground and spin her around.

When I set her down, my heart is beating rapidly. Not from the exertion of lifting her up, but because she hasn't said anything about *us* yet.

But she's here, in my apartment.

She brushes her fingers over my forehead. "You had some dirt there."

"I was saving it for you. Sexy, isn't it?"

She laughs, and then her expression sobers. "I'm sorry I put you through that break. After my interview, I realized something." She swallows. "I thought I had to be perfect to be with you."

I frown. "I don't have a fancy job, or make a lot of money, or—"

"I don't care about those things, and I always liked how you're secure in who you are. Don't start lacking in confidence now."

"I'm not." I mean, the greatest woman in the world has come back me. I'm feeling pretty good about myself.

"What I'm trying to say, Peter." She twists her hands together. "Is that you're just right for *me*. From the very beginning, you've been so good to me. I don't really believe in things like fate, but I'd just made up a boyfriend named Peter to please my mother, and then you showed up and agreed to my ridiculous fake-boyfriend proposal."

"I already liked you. I asked you out first."

"And I shot you down."

"Yeah, and I jumped at the chance to get to know you better. It was only sensible."

She puts her hands on my shoulders. "You've helped me feel like myself again. You've helped me *feel* again, because when I'm with you, I'm safe; I can handle anything. Every moment we've spent together, whether I was chasing you around with a durian bun or dancing with you in a bar...I loved all of it.

"Although I was scared because of what my other relationship was like, I was also overwhelmed, since this is so different from what I experienced before. A part of me thought I had to be some perfect version of myself before I could tell you how I feel, because you're so perfect for me. But I already am that person when I'm with you, regardless of whether or not I have my perfect life. From now on, I want us to be together."

I clear my throat. "That's lucky," I say, my voice a bit rough, "because that's what I want, too. I want to be with you when it's good, and when it's bad. I don't want you to feel like you have to take a break from me so you can figure things out on your own. I'm with you, every step of the way. I know you're going to do amazing things in life, but I also know that not everything will go exactly the way you want it—there are always stumbling blocks. Whatever happens, I admire you so much."

"I didn't think I could do this again," she whispers. "A boyfriend—I didn't even want to think about it, and I couldn't imagine trying to go back to software development. But you made it possible. The way you make me feel..." She shakes her head. "I love you, Peter. I realized it the last time I saw you, and it made me want to run, but I can say it now. I love you. It still scares me a little, but I'm getting used to it, and like I said, you make me feel safe. Although that might sound like no big deal, for me, it's everything. I think I needed the fake relationship to ease myself into the idea, but it's very real now, and I'm happy."

I touch her tear-stained cheeks and her lips, curved up in a tentative smile.

"I'm glad," I say. "I love you, too. You and your inexplicable fondness for durian make me feel something I've never felt in a past relationship, and I know I want this to last."

She wipes more tears from her cheeks. "My God, this isn't like me."

"I'm here for every version of you."

And then, because I can't wait any longer, I kiss her.

We were already standing so close, but now I wrap my arms around her, and she squeaks as I lift her up and kiss her lips. A kiss that I hope says "I love you," and so many other things I can't articulate.

"Alright," she says, breathless as I set her down, "we should eat some of this food."

"I did notice there was an awful lot of food."

"I tried to buy everything we've eaten together." She frowns. "Maybe it's excessive—I don't know how to do romantic gestures—but we can eat the leftovers for the next week. I'll stay here with you, if that's okay. I brought my suitcase." She gestures to the corner.

I clasp her hand in mine as we walk to the kitchen. There's Japanese cheesecake, potato pancake with kimchi jjigae, pupusas, flourless chocolate cake, lamb skewers, noodles ...

So many memories run through my mind as I look at all the food.

And then there's a durian bun.

"I'll let you eat that one by yourself," I say.

Valerie and I are very different, and not just in our feelings about durian. I'm easygoing; she's more intense. She's an introvert; I'm an extrovert. She has a career that means a lot to her; I just want a job with a decent salary that allows me to live my life.

But we fit together wonderfully. We complement each other.

"There's also ice cream in the fridge," she says. "Just stuff from Ginger Scoops. No Thai rolled ice cream."

"I went to that place the other day," I admit. "Because I missed you so much."

"Oh, Peter. I'm sorry."

"It's okay. You told me you'd come back to me, and you did."

I fill my plate with noodles and pupusas, and as we eat, we talk about the future.

"I'm going to move out," Valerie says. "I'll start looking for apartments right away and hopefully find something in the next month or two."

"You could live with me."

"I figured you might say that." She stuffs some potato pancake in her mouth. "But I've never lived alone, and I want to do that for at least a year. Then maybe we can think about getting a place together, something a little bigger than this."

"Sure." I smile at her. "We should probably also think about telling your family that I'm not a doctor."

"Oh, my mom already knows. She came home from mahjong at two in the morning, yelling about how you'd been lying to me. You know how her friend's niece was in your supposed year in med school? Well, she asked around, and nobody knew a Peter So, and she found your profile on Facebook." She pauses. "For a while, I was convinced there had to be something wrong with you. After everything that happened to me last year, this seemed too amazing to be real. That's why I wanted to talk to

Deepti alone, but she said you were a good guy. When my mom said you were lying...I figured, that was it. But it was just the lie about you being a pediatrician, which *I* told you to do."

"How did she react?"

"Well, she was glad you hadn't been lying to me. She'd probably like you a tiny bit more if you were actually a pediatrician, but she's happy for me." Valerie squeezes my hand. "I'm sorry I doubted you. It had nothing to do with how you've acted with me. I just..."

"I understand. I admit I was a bit annoyed after you talked to Deepti, but I knew why you were doing it."

She squeezes my hand again. "This isn't too amazing to be real, and I can accept that now, I promise. I trust you. It's difficult for me, but I do. When I spilled my durian ice cream on you, I never would have imagined this happening."

Yes, it turns out that durian—specifically, durian ice cream—can lead to something great. Perhaps it's not my nemesis after all.

I agreed to her fake-boyfriend plan partly for the novelty of it, and I got way more than that, though I did get a great story, too. One day I'll tell it at our wedding, but there's still some time before we get to that point.

I look at Valerie, with her glorious smile and her long dark hair framing her face, and I'm blown away by how lucky I am.

I think it might be time to show her...in bed.

She squeezes my hand. "By the way, what was in the box you were carrying when you came in?"

"Ah. Perfect timing, actually." I grab the box from the hall and open it up. There's another box inside.

"The vibrator!" She puts her hands to her mouth. "I'd totally forgotten."

"Want to try it out now?"

She glances at all the food on the table. "Well…"

"We can have dessert afterward."

"Good idea.

"We can alternate between sex and dessert all night. One orgasm, then a slice of Japanese cheesecake. Two more orgasms, then a durian bun for you—and flourless chocolate cake for me. Another orgasm…"

She kisses me on the lips and leads me to the bedroom, where I make quick work of her clothes and give her all the pleasure I can.

She's mine, and I'm hers, and I couldn't ask for anything more.

Epilogue

Valerie

The following summer...

"WHERE ARE WE GOING?" I ask as I fasten my seatbelt.

"You'll see." Peter leans over and kisses me on the cheek. "Happy birthday, sweetheart."

To be honest, I'm ninety percent sure of the answer to my question. It's a little shop tucked in a plaza in the suburbs, and I'm super excited.

It might not be the most romantic place in the world, but I don't care.

I'm going to eat durian!

He places his hand on my thigh as we start driving north. It's a hot July day, and I'm wearing a pink skirt with a white blouse. I think I look pretty good, and—

"You look amazing," he says.

I smile.

We lapse into a comfortable silence for several minutes. I open my window and breathe in the warm summer air.

I met Peter about ten months ago, and those ten months have been amazing. Eight months ago, I started my new job in software development. Although it was a bit of an adjustment at first, I'm happy with how things are going now, and I recently got a promotion. I don't think I want to work for my friend's boyfriend's company forever, but I feel like I have options, and I'm excited about the future. at all

I live in my own apartment downtown, within walking distance of Peter's apartment. We spend a few nights together every week, but I've enjoyed living on my own for the first time.

Soon, however, we'll start looking for a place to live together. He also said something about taking me shopping for engagement rings, and I think I'm ready.

I don't know exactly what the future will bring, but it's been great to have him by my side this year. This fall, we're going to Europe for a couple of weeks, which will be our first big vacation together. I can't wait.

We'll probably have kids one day, though not for at least a few years. Peter has talked about being a stay-at-home dad until the kids start school, which is cool with me. I think he'll be a great father, and I have no interest in staying home beyond my maternity leave.

But for now, it's just us.

Every time he looks at me, I can see love in his eyes. A year ago, I would have scoffed at the thought, but it's true.

We're in Richmond Hill now, and sure enough, the plaza where he brought me last fall—and a few times since—comes into view.

I bounce in my seat. "I knew it."

When we get out of the car, he takes my hand and leads me to Doctor Durian. There are a couple of new things on the menu, but I stick with my favorite: durian pancakes, plus a small durian shake. Peter orders the mango pancakes.

"Just like the first time we came here," I say.

We sit on the lone rickety table outside, right next to the parking lot.

"I'm never going to like durian," he says, "but I've developed an odd fondness for its natural gas, rotten onion, and vomit smell."

"Oh really?"

"Whenever I smell it, I know you're going to smile, and that makes me happy."

Peter is the sweetest.

After we've finished our food and I'm sipping the last of my durian shake, he hands me a cream-colored envelope. Inside is a red card with a small cut-out of a durian on the front. When I open it, a durian pops up.

"I love it!" I can't believe he managed to find a durian pop-up card.

"I had this theory, not long after we met," he says, "that you were like a durian. Because you're spiky on the outside and mushy on the inside, and utterly delicious."

I can't help rolling my eyes. "But you don't like durian."

"Nah, but you do. I look at you...the way you look at a durian."

"You're much better than durian. And that's a very big compliment, coming from me."

With Peter, I'm living the life I want. So much different from a year ago.

After I finish my durian shake, we go for a walk in Sherwood Park, and then we meet Chloe, Sarah, Drew, and Josh at the Chinese restaurant we went to last fall, the one with lamb and hand-pulled noodles.

My friends hug me and wish me happy birthday. Business at Ginger Scoops has picked up, and Chloe's hired someone to replace me, as well as a high school student to help out during the summer. It's easier for her to get away from the shop for the occasional evening now.

Chloe, Sarah, and I are all doing well. A year ago, Chloe had found Drew and Sarah had found Josh, and I was convinced that love could happen for my friends, but it wasn't something that could happen for me.

I was wrong.

I met an incredible guy, and I trust him completely.

His hand finds mine under the table, and a frisson of heat runs through me at the simple touch. Later, he'll take me to bed, but for now...

He pours us all some tea, and I raise my little teacup, as though in a toast. Unfortunately, I can't think of anything to say. This is embarrassing.

Peter saves me. He knocks his cup against mine. "To Valerie," he says simply.

Everyone joins in, and my cheeks flush, just a little, as they all look at me.

Did you know there are durian buffets? Yes, such things exist—I recently read about one in Malaysia. But right now, at a restaurant in Toronto with my boyfriend and friends, I'd say I'm luckier than a durian lover at a durian buffet.

True story.

About the Author

Jackie Lau decided she wanted to be a writer when she was in grade two, sometime between writing "The Heart That Got Lost" and "The Land of Shapes." She later studied engineering and worked as a geophysicist before turning to writing romance novels. Jackie lives in Toronto with her husband, and despite living in Canada her whole life, she hates winter. When she's not writing, she enjoys gelato, gourmet donuts, cooking, hiking, and reading on the balcony when it's raining.

To learn more and sign up for her newsletter,
visit jackielaubooks.com.

Also by Jackie Lau

Love, Lies, and Cherry Pie

Time Loops & Meet Cutes

Donut Fall in Love Series
Donut Fall in Love
The Stand-Up Groomsman

Weddings with the Moks Series
Four Weddings to Fall in Love
Three Reasons to Run
Two Friends in Marriage

Baldwin Village Series
One Bed for Christmas (prequel novella)
The Ultimate Pi Day Party
Ice Cream Lover
Man vs. Durian

Chu's Restaurant Series

The Sitcom Star
The Reluctant Heartthrob

Kwan Sisters/Fong Brothers Series

Grumpy Fake Boyfriend
Mr. Hotshot CEO
Pregnant by the Playboy
Bidding for the Bachelor

Cider Bar Sisters Series

Her Big City Neighbor
His Grumpy Childhood Friend
Her Pretend Christmas Date (novella)
The Professor Next Door
Her Favorite Rebound
Her Unexpected Roommate

Holidays with the Wongs Series

A Match Made for Thanksgiving
A Second Chance Road Trip for Christmas
A Fake Girlfriend for Chinese New Year
A Big Surprise for Valentine's Day

Chin-Williams Series

Not Another Family Wedding
He's Not My Boyfriend

www.ingramcontent.com/pod-product-compliance
Lightning Source LLC
Chambersburg PA
CBHW021134190726
48288CB00008B/2650